Tell My Dad

Ram Muthiah

Waimea
Publishing

Published in 2016 by Waimea Publishing

Library of Congress Control Number: 2016936705

ISBN: 978-0-9973906-6-7

Editors: CreateSpace Team, Donna Rich, Ramya R, Lisa Z; Proofreader: Donna Rich; Cover Design: Denis Lenzi

Author's Note

This book is inspired by a tragic event that happened in California, where a five-year-old girl was kidnapped because of her kindness in helping strangers. The girl's friend helped the cops track the kidnapper. However, the cruel man had killed the innocent child in a gruesome way before the cops could track him down. That incident, combined with seemingly never-ending Amber Alerts, motivated me to write this book.

Although inspired by true events, this story is a work of fiction.

Dedication

To all children who were taken away from their families

Chapter 1

Amanda Rivera, December 18

Because of the rush of excitement, Amanda Rivera felt more like flying than driving as her Honda sedan cruised on El Camino Real South. Exactly twenty minutes earlier, she had read the acceptance email from Stanford. She was jubilant and screamed with joy when she realized that the university had confirmed MST, her requested major. MST covered music, science, and technology. She was passionate about music. She was also madly in love with technology. It seemed that most teenagers who lived in the San Francisco Bay Area were seriously thinking of starting the next social media venture or the next Google. It may have been the water in Silicon Valley or the positive entrepreneurial vibe emanating from Apple headquarters in Cupertino.

Amanda was a senior at an all-girls Catholic school in Burlingame. She had loved music since she first started learning piano in the San Mateo Cultural Center at the age of eleven. She loved to go to all the music festivals in the San Francisco Bay Area and daydreamed about releasing an album. Her bedroom wall was fully covered with posters of Taylor Swift and Selena Gomez—just like many other teenagers. However, there was one difference. In the middle of the room, she had a poster of herself with the Grammy Award in hand, thanks to her photoshopping skills.

In a Catholic school, no one could escape religion class. It was a boring one for most of the girls, but not for Amanda. She loved the message of compassion and synergy. She also loved the fact that her music teacher, Ms. Ramirez, taught religion class as well. Ms. Ramirez turned boring religion lectures into musicals. Instead of making them memorize Bible verses, she composed rhyming songs by fusing the scripture with music theory. She was the guiding angel for Amanda. Whenever Amanda was down, she was always there for her, encouraging her and cheering her up. She preached "what you think is what you become," and then gave the photoshop idea to Amanda and asked her to visualize herself every day holding the Grammy Award in her hand. It seemed to be working!

Amanda was grateful to Ms. Ramirez for another reason—proposing a policy to the school board to collaborate with the all-boys Catholic school in Burlingame for their annual theatrical performance. That policy helped Amanda to meet her sweetheart.

Amanda was a junior when she met Billy for the first time in her choir classroom during the rehearsal. They rehearsed along with twenty other students every weekend for a month. As per the original plan, Amanda was going to sing a solo and Billy would play the piano solo. God bless Ms. Ramirez. Just before the live event, she got the wonderful idea of having them do a duet, which was a hit. It also made them fall madly in love with each other. It had been almost nine months since Billy had declared that he could not live without Amanda. However, Amanda felt like she had known him for a very, very long time.

Two weeks earlier, Billy had told Amanda that it was possible that they were Pyramus and Thisbe in ancient times and had been reborn again to continue where they had left off. Amanda laughed nonstop when she heard that the first time.

"How do you come up with this kind of lame idea?"

"This is not lame, you know. It is very possible. I feel a strong connection when I sit next to you."

"*Really*? Are all boys like this? This is how you guys trick girls?"

"Oh, Amanda! You think I am tricking you. I sense something powerful. Maybe we were not Pyramus and Thisbe, but there is something!"

Amanda smiled as she remembered Billy's romantic gesture. She took a sharp right into Hillsdale Mall's parking lot. It was eleven o'clock on Friday morning. Traffic around the mall was not bad. She drove the car to the parking lot closer to Sears and found a space. Sometimes, getting a parking space was like winning the mega million lottery.

Amanda jumped out of the car, clicked the remote to lock the car, and walked across a small lane to enter Sears. She was still on top of the world; Stanford admission was surreal.

Earlier in the day, she had called Billy as soon as she read the acceptance email. He did not answer. So she left a voicemail. "Hey, Pyramus, call me back ASAP. I have important news!" without revealing the good news; she loved to keep him in suspense.

Inside the store, she related every object she looked at to the college dorm room she imagined. When she passed through the appliance section, she wondered whether Stanford dorm rooms had microwaves. Her mind raced with the questions about the kind of room she would get in the university housing: single or double. She made a mental note to ask the housing people for a double room as she crossed the furniture section.

As she moved up on the escalator, she sent a text message. "Hey, lazy. Call now." She waited for thirty seconds. Then, she sent another one.

After grabbing a couple of pairs of jeans, lots of tees, and two tall red mugs with Stanford University's logo, she waited for a long time in the checkout line. It was pretty obvious that the woman at the checkout counter hated her job. *No wonder Sears is closing shops.* While waiting, she checked her phone every minute to see if there was a reply from Billy. Nothing. *What happened to him?*

Amanda came out of the store holding paper bags in both hands and walked toward the car. It was noon. The weather was nice although it seemed warmer than usual. The parking lot was sparsely occupied. A few people walked toward the store as she crossed the small lane in front of Sears to enter the open parking lot. She was more excited than she could ever remember and wondered for the tenth time how Billy would react to her Stanford news. She was just a few feet away from her blue Honda Civic when she noticed something odd.

A tall man, about six-foot-six, wearing a dark T-shirt and dark sunglasses stepped in front of her and grabbed her right hand tightly.

Panic set in. She thought someone was trying to steal her

bag. Immediately, she shouted, "Help! Thief!"

The man tightened his grip and pulled her into the Lexus SUV parked to his left. Then, he slapped her face and pushed her inside through the back door, which was held open. She lost the grip on her bags and let those fall on the concrete floor next to the muddy wheel of the Lexus.

Her head bumped into the back of the headrest and rested on the backseat. She smelled rotten leather for a second. Then, she quickly bounced back and tried hard to push him away. She screamed from the top of her lungs, "Help! Help! Help!"

As she tried to push the ferocious man away and get out of the vehicle, she spotted an old couple walking behind the Lexus, looking confused. The woman gasped and looked at her husband, who stood speechless. The tall man came toward Amanda with something in his hand. She screamed again, crouched, pushed into his stomach, and emerged from the vehicle. He grabbed her hair with one hand, placed a small towel in her nose, and pushed her into the backseat. The chloroform-soaked towel fully covered her nose now. She saw herself holding a Grammy Award at MetLife stadium in Los Angeles. Then, the stadium went dark.

Chapter 2

Patricia Gonzalo clenched her chest as she watched the Lexus SUV speed away from the parking lot. *What just happened?*

"Oh my lord! Did you see that? Did that man kidnap that girl?" She squinted her eyes and stared at her husband, who held their grandson's hands tight.

"I don't know. Call 911. What is this world coming to?" Mark Gonzalo was visibly shaken.

Five minutes later, at twelve past noon, two young police officers arrived at the scene. One was tall and big with lots of hair and a curly mustache. The other one was about five-foot-four, with a goatee and eyeglasses.

Patricia had trouble breathing. She could not forgive herself for what she did not do. "I'm sorry, Officers. We didn't know someone could do this in broad daylight. For a second, we thought these kids were just fighting. We didn't know whether we should get involved."

The officer with a curly mustache said, "Don't worry,

ma'am. No one would have expected a kidnapping here in an open parking lot. Don't be hard on yourself. We will find the girl. Did you notice the license plate?" He was ready to note down the details.

Patricia sighed. "Gosh…How did we not see that? It was a Lexus SUV, light green, kind of faded green. Old car. It did not occur to me to note the license plate. It all happened so quick!"

The young boy raised his hand and said, "Grandma, I saw the license plate."

The officer noted down the license plate details as Patricia looked at her grandson with pride.

The officer with the goatee knelt down and examined the paper bags lying on the floor. He looked up and asked, "This is where the SUV was parked, right?"

Patricia came forward and nodded. "Little further to the right."

The officer pulled the wallet out from the paper bag. He opened it and found the driver's license. He signaled Patricia to come closer and showed her the picture on the license. "This is the girl you saw, right?"

Patricia nodded sadly. She felt sweat over her entire body and pain in her heart. She glanced at her husband, who sat on the concrete, cross-legged with his hands on his bald head. She adjusted her pink top, placed her hands on her hips, and spoke in a louder voice. "Mark, get up now. This is not the place for you to faint. We need to go and find that girl."

Mark looked up.

Patricia continued, "I told you a long time ago. We need to get that damned pepper spray."

~

Samantha Cruz was busy finishing up her criminology assignment. She was supposed to write a three-page essay about serial killers and their motivations. She got distracted and annoyed when her mother kept switching channels on the television.

"Hey, Mom, just make up your mind and stick to one channel," chided Samantha.

"Do you think the guy who invented the remote is an idiot? He knew that we can't watch one channel for five minutes."

"Mom! I can't focus with all this noise. I need to finish this damn thing."

"Watch your language, Samantha," she said in a stern voice. "Go to your room and study. The living room is meant for TV."

Just then, both Samantha and her mother looked at the television screen, which flashed "A seventeen-year-old girl was kidnapped from Hillsdale Mall parking lot at noon." Samantha looked at her mother, who was instantly shaken.

"Oh my God, someone kidnapped her in broad daylight? No one was there to save the girl?"

For the next fifteen minutes, her mother was glued to the screen. Samantha had witnessed the tragedy parents had to go through when she volunteered for the National Center for Missing Children a few years earlier during her junior year in high school. Her heart and mind started racing. She looked at her mother and said, "Whoever kidnapped that girl won't be able to hide for very long. You know, cops can draw a sketch of the man just by talking to witnesses."

Her mother stared at the television screen in horror. She said nothing.

•

Chapter 3

Manuel Bracamontes pulled the Lexus into the garage, shut the door, and looked around. The garage was littered with cardboard boxes, chainsaws, and tools. He opened the backdoor of the vehicle and found the girl, who was in a deep sleep. The chloroform was doing its job. He patted his shoulder in pride before carrying the girl inside the house.

A minute later, he stood inside the bedroom, holding her in his arms. He felt like he was holding a Vince Lombardi trophy. He stared at her face for a few seconds. *Sleeping beauty.*

He looked up and checked the time on the analog clock on the wall. Twenty-two minutes past noon. It would take at least one more hour before the girl would regain consciousness. He gently placed her on the queen-sized bed and adjusted the pillow to properly support her head. He jumped off the bed, stared at her one more time, closed the bedroom door, walked quickly toward the garage, and backed the Lexus into the street.

Three minutes later, he drove the Lexus to the corner

of Laurelwood Lane and Sylvan Avenue. Then, he parked the vehicle in the small lane behind a Chinese restaurant and walked toward Laurelwood Park. There, he jumped inside a green Volvo, turned the engine on, and drove toward his house.

~

Jack Ackerman's phone rang as he watched his three-year-old daughter, Rebecca, giggling and sliding down the elephant-shaped plastic slide in Laurelwood Park with both hands up. The park had been built in the seventies. It was popular among residents and was always packed during weekends. There were not many people around on Friday morning except for a few parents, who were pushing their children in strollers.

Officer Walker was on the phone. "Lieutenant, there was a kidnapping, seventeen-year-old girl, in Hillsdale parking lot."

"That's insane. In broad daylight? From a mall parking lot?"

"Yeah. It happened ten minutes ago. Captain asked me to check to see if you're available." He quickly added, "It's okay if you have other plans."

Ackerman immediately answered, "I'll be there soon. I just need to check with my wife about where to drop off my daughter."

Ackerman sighed as he hung up. It was supposed to be a day off and a long weekend. He looked at Rebecca, who was running from one slide to another before dialing the number.

"Hey, seventeen-year-old was kidnapped in the parking

lot in Hillsdale Mall…Yeah, just now. Captain asked me to come in." He leaned against his Ford and looked around as he listened to his wife. "Sounds good. Thanks for understanding. I'll drop Rebecca at your sister's place and head to the station."

As he clicked the end button on the phone, he saw a man nervously walking across the street. He kept looking around. For a second, Ackerman thought the man was going to cause some trouble. However, he got into a green Volvo parked closer to the park entrance and drove off without creating a scene, like a good citizen.

Manuel shut the garage door behind himself and walked across the living room to grab two beer bottles from the refrigerator. He wiped the sweat from his forehead and whistled as he made dance movements with the bottles in both hands. *Time for a celebration.* He slid onto the couch facing the television in the living room, stretched his legs on the Moroccan wool ottoman, and gulped beer as he switched on the television. *What a day!*

A proud smile formed on his face when he saw the news headlines. He raised the empty beer bottle in his right hand and said loudly, "Breaking news! I am breaking news today, baby!"

It was a thrilling experience, rather an adventure, to kidnap the girl in public view. He watched the news anchor speculating about how the kidnapper might have rehearsed it many times to carry out the act. He smirked and pointed his finger at the news anchor. "Really? Do you guys know I pulled it off just like that?"

He had been awake until four o'clock in the morning

chatting in an underground Internet forum. During the nightly chat sessions with like-minded strangers, he was intrigued by a forum thread in which someone, masked by the username "horseman," wanted handlers to kidnap girls in the Bay Area. Manuel had engaged in a good number of criminal activities in the past. But kidnapping was not one of them.

When he woke up at ten o'clock, the first thing that came to his mind was kidnapping a girl. *Why not try that?* While sipping a latte in a coffee shop in Hillsdale Mall, a few blocks from his house, he brainstormed a kidnapping strategy.

While walking back home, he saw the uncovered parking lot outside Sears. It was pretty big, but there weren't many cars. On the other side of the road, there was a furniture shop. The parking lot and the furniture shop were separated by El Camino Real, a four-lane road with a big median in the middle. It would be difficult for anyone from the furniture shop to spot someone quickly grabbing a girl.

He had hatched a perfect plan by the time he reached home. He took a quick shower and drove his grandma's beat-up Volvo to Laurelwood Park. After parking it near the park entrance, he roamed around the smaller lanes of the park area looking for the perfect vehicle to steal. He found an older model Lexus behind a Chinese restaurant in a small lane. It took him less than five minutes to hotwire the engine and another five minutes to drive it to the mall parking lot.

When he saw Amanda jumping out of her car so full of life, he decided that she was *the girl*. He had never seen anyone that happy. The girl's enthusiasm and bright smile mesmerized him. He waited until she entered Sears and took a spot next to her car. Then, he waited.

His plan was simple and lethal. Let the girl walk to the

car, surprise her, and grab her before she realized what was going on. He calculated that even if other people saw it, they would not realize what was going on at least for a few minutes. That time would be enough for him to drive through a small street behind Sears and head to his house down Sylvan Avenue.

So far, Manuel's plan had worked just fine. No one could locate him. No one would have noticed the license plate of the SUV he drove. Even if someone noticed it, the cops would spend hours harassing the poor guy who owned that vehicle.

He planned the getaway and had chosen the route with no traffic cameras. He abandoned the stolen vehicle and switched to his vehicle seamlessly. It was all pretty quick. Now, he could keep the girl in the house for *years* before anyone found out.

He stopped staring at the beer bottle and looked at the television screen when the news anchor talked about the missing girl and the license plate of the vehicle that was used in the kidnapping. The girl's picture flashed on the screen. The picture did not do justice to her beauty.

He switched off the television, trashed the empty beer bottles, and entered the bathroom, which was right behind the couch.

∾

The San Mateo Police Department's situation room was bristling with activity. Captain Sheldon stared through the window at the group of children walking into the Whole Foods store across the street and waited for the train horn from the nearby Caltrain station to subside before addressing the officers standing in front of him.

"We have the girl's picture. We have the license plate of the vehicle. An Amber Alert has already been issued. A sketch artist is working with the witnesses. Once we have the sketch, we will release it to the press. Unfortunately, the witnesses had only a partial view of the suspect's face." He paused for a second and said, "The FBI has been notified. They're on the way."

He shook his head in disbelief. "What the hell was this asshole thinking? Kidnap a girl in broad daylight with people looking?" He looked at Officer Walker. "Did you get anything from traffic cameras?"

"He didn't come out of the mall. We have cameras on both sides of El Camino. There was no Lexus SUV coming out of the mall in the last thirty minutes. We're reviewing the tapes again."

"He might have taken roads behind the mall. Do we have any cameras on Thirty-First Avenue?"

"We do. We checked that too and got nothing."

"Okay. He can't hide unless—"

"Unless what?"

"If he had a place to hide between the mall and the freeway. There are so many small streets, behind the mall. There are no traffic cameras. He could have planned that route." Captain Sheldon bunched his right hand into a fist and struck the wooden desk. "I'm pissed off, seriously pissed off. Kidnapping at noon in public view? It's an insult to all of us."

Chapter 4

Manuel came out of the shower wearing a plush bathrobe and abruptly stopped when he heard the television news anchors talking about the abduction. He wiped off his face with the towel and frowned at the television. He remembered switching it off before entering the shower. *Something is wrong.* He threw the towel on the couch, quickly walked over to the bedroom, and opened the door. The girl was still sleeping.

As he sighed and closed the bedroom door slowly, he felt a sharp pain in his neck and lost his grip on the doorknob. He quickly looked over his left shoulder as he fell on his right on the hardwood floor. A monk with a shaved head, a round face, blue eyes, a sharp nose, and a red monastic robe stood tall.

Manuel's adrenaline pumped up as he quickly stood up. He scanned to his left, searched for a knife on the dining table, and found none. His hip hurt from the fall.

"Who are you?" he shouted.

The monk stood still and signaled for him to come closer.

Manuel ground his teeth, shook his head, cursed, and lurched forward to beat the monk to death.

The monk quickly moved into action. He grabbed Manuel's arm and shoulder firmly and pushed his right forearm against Manuel's neck. Then, the monk pulled Manuel's body forward and down while bringing his right knee up. The monk's knee went hard and fast at a horizontal angle. He slammed his right knee first into Manuel's ribs, then his stomach, and then his head.

When the monk finished his first round of knee strikes, Manuel felt intense pain and blood gushing from his nose, which added a good amount of confusion to the surprising attack. The monk did not stop. He continued to strike Manuel by keeping his firm grip on his right arm and shoulder. After three strikes, in a desperate attempt, Manuel grabbed the monk's neck and choked him, which made the monk let go of his shoulder.

In a split second, the monk's right palm moved at forty miles per hour and landed a powerful strike on Manuel's chin, which caused his bottom middle teeth to separate from the gum.

Then, the monk quickly pulled back his right arm, rotated his left shoulder inward and upward, raised his right arm toward Manuel's right cheekbone, and drove his legs upward to add power to the punch.

Manuel screamed after losing two more teeth.

The monk pulled back and delivered a straight punch to Manuel's chest.

Manuel fell on the couch on his butt, closed his eyes, and cried in pain.

The monk pulled rubber gloves, nylon rope, and duct tape from his red-colored mountain backpack and tied Manuel's hands and legs with the rope before wrapping the duct tape around his mouth. Then, he grabbed the remote lying on the floor and pointed it at the television.

News anchors were seriously debating how long it would take to find the dead body of the girl in a typical kidnapping case. The monk shook his head, clicked his tongue, and switched off the television.

He walked to his right and slowly opened the bedroom door. He scanned the bedroom and the back of the bedroom door quickly to make sure there was no threat. Then, he gently walked toward the girl sleeping on the bed and checked her pulse. *The girl is alive, thank God.*

He scanned the living room as he closed the bedroom door. To his left was a filthy-looking kitchen with a small dining table and two chairs. On his right was the big living room with the couch in the middle. The house was silent except for the muffled moan coming from the man on the couch.

He quickly walked over to the kitchen and searched for something before spotting the faded blue jeans hanging on the dining chair. He searched the jeans pockets and retrieved a phone and a cigarette lighter. Then, he walked back to the couch, rolled the spark wheel of the lighter, and pointed the flame directly below Manuel's clean-shaven chin.

He heard Manuel's scream, loud and clear in spite of duct tape muffling it. He pointed his gun at Manuel. "Do you hear me?"

Manuel nodded.

"Good. I'm going to ask you a couple of questions. If you lie, I will kill you right here." He removed the duct tape from Manuel's mouth and maintained three feet of distance. He held his gun steady and pointed it at Manuel's forehead.

"Did you think the cops would never find you?"

"You're a cop?" Manuel did not like his own question.

"I hate people answering questions with a question. Let's do this again. What is the plan?"

"I don't know. Why the hell do you care?"

"Have you ever thought about what the parents go through when a girl is taken by assholes like you?" He waved his gun at the bedroom door.

"Oh shit. You're the father?"

"Yes. I am." He did not show any emotion as he calmly placed the silencer on the mouth of the gun.

"Hey, stop…" Manuel shook his head vigorously and struggled for the words. "I will do whatever you want. Take the girl. Okay? It was just supposed to be fun and adventure, man!" He lowered his head after failing to meet the monk's intense gaze. "How did you find me?" He stared at the nylon rope that kept his wrists together.

"I could have stopped you in Sears. I was following you to see if there are other guys involved. It's time to end your *adventure*."

A second later, the monk pulled the trigger. A bullet went into the center of Manuel's forehead, took a little tour inside his skull, and came out behind the sofa. Bullet casings hit the hardwood floor and created a mild ding.

The monk removed the duct tape and nylon rope and stuffed those in his backpack. Then, he scanned the living room and front door before checking Manuel's pulse to make sure he was dead.

The monk took a deep breath, cocked his head to the right, and stared at the dead man on the couch. He pulled out the Glock he had shoved inside his robe and shot Manuel one more time between his legs. He paused for a second. Then, he shot him multiple times between his legs, until he emptied the chamber.

Next, he took out a small machine, a portable voice changer, from his backpack. He connected one end of the voice changer to Manuel's phone, dialed 911, and started speaking to the operator. After a few minutes of conversation with the clueless young lady on the other side, he placed the phone next to Manuel's dead body. Then, he calmly walked away and opened the front door before pulling up his hood. He put his head down, turned to his left, and walked toward Sylvan Avenue before climbing into a Honda Odyssey parked in the far corner. Then, he waited to hear police sirens.

Chapter 5

Ackerman and Walker looked at each other when they heard the voice emanating from the police radio. "All units respond. We have the location of Amanda Rivera." Walker listened to the address and sped up without speaking a word.

Ackerman continued to listen to the message coming through the police radio. Someone had called 911 and left a short message after giving the location of the girl. "Bad guy is dead. Justice is done. Send an ambulance. The girl is alive but sedated."

They reached the house in less than five minutes and saw a few officers at the front gate of the house. Two teenagers from the neighboring house gazed at the officers, who were walking around the house with their guns drawn.

Ackerman walked quickly into the house. He saw the man in the plush bathrobe sitting on the couch; his dead eyes faced the ceiling.

"The guy is dead. He was shot multiple times," an officer

said.

Ackerman did not hear that. He was staring at the writing on the forehead of the dead guy.

"*Stay away.*" Two words were written using black permanent marker with a bullet hole in between.

Down below the waist, the man's bathrobe was soaked in blood.

"No shit. *That* must have caused some serious pain," Walker said as he pointed at the dead man's genital area.

Ackerman nodded. "This is an overkill. Personal. Deep. The killer may be related to the girl." He turned around and scanned the house for signs of the girl.

"The girl's still asleep in the bedroom. She's heavily sedated. An ambulance is on the way," the officer said.

"No one else in the house?"

"Nope. We searched the entire house."

"Check the bathrooms. Backyard as well. The killer must be somewhere close by."

Ackerman stared again at the graffiti on the dead man's forehead. In less than a week, two people had been killed in San Mateo. The killer had written the same warning on the forehead.

He ran his right hand through his hair as he watched the blood streak on the hardwood floor. The guy on the couch had been dragged from the bedroom to the couch. *Did the killer kill him before dragging him?*

He watched Walker pulling a wallet out from the jeans hanging on the dining chair.

"His name is, um—*was* Manuel Bracamontes." Walker waved the driver's license.

Ackerman looked closely. "We need to find out everything about this guy. This is similar to the killing in the Delaware apartment on Sunday. There may be a connection between these two murders. The FBI is on their way. Their CARD team should know that there is a killer out there who is doing their job."

Chapter 6

Maria Winters, December 29

Shannon Winters adjusted her dress, straightened the hair falling over her forehead, and checked the handbag one more time. Then, she walked over to Maria's room and knocked on the door.

"I'm heading out to the hospital. I locked the back door. Make sure you lock the dead bolt on the front door. Be safe, okay?"

"Don't worry, Mom. I'm not a baby anymore. I'm fifteen!" Maria got up from the red gaming chair, which she used for playing Halo on the Xbox mounted below the twenty-inch LED monitor.

Shannon hugged her. "Well, you're still a baby to me! Be safe. Call me if you need anything." She watched Maria nodding and following her to the front door.

"Don't forget. Lock the dead bolt."

"How can I forget when you tell me that a hundred times?" Maria giggled as she locked the door. She watched through the window as her mother backed her Nissan Altima down the driveway.

As soon as her mother's car disappeared from her view, she ran to her room, brought the laptop to life, and logged on to Facebook. She quickly checked if Justin was online. His status was offline. She looked at the right bottom corner of her laptop screen. The computer clock indicated it was 9:00 p.m.

The web page changed Justin's status from "Offline" to "Mobile" with a green dot next to it.

Her hormones surged, and her eyes lit up. She quickly typed, "Hi!!! Just got here?" and added multiple smiley emoticons in sequence.

"Hey, Maria! You seem to be in a very good mood! I kept my word. I'm here sharply at nine! Just like I said!!"

"Yeah, you are a man of your word!"

"I am. You seem to be really happy today!"

"Of course. My mom just left for the hospital."

"Oh yes! I remember, your mom is a nurse in Mills Peninsula, right?"

"Yep! She won't be back until 7:00 a.m. We can chat all night!!!"

"Awesome! What are you wearing?"

She blushed. "What am I wearing? Who wants to know? You naughty... :-)" She heard some rattling noise coming from the backyard as she added more emoticons to the chat window. *What is that noise?*

She ignored the noise and focused on typing. "I'm not telling. You guess."

"My guess will be pretty wild!" Justin replied.

She bit her lips, smiled, and thought about how to respond to his mischievous comment. Then, she heard the rattling noise again.

"I think the raccoons are back. Let me check. Hold on." She got to her feet without waiting for the reply.

A big raccoon had gotten in last Sunday. Maria was so scared when she saw the raccoon coming into the kitchen. Her mother had been there to take care of it. Now, Maria started to worry. She checked the kitchen window. There was nothing. All the windows were tightly sealed. It was totally dark outside. She could hear only the sound of the wind now.

She sighed and went back to her laptop. "Hey, handsome, r u there?"

There was no reply.

She heard the rattling noise again, but it was a little louder than it had been earlier. "Oh, not again." She cursed the raccoons of the world and looked to where the sound was coming from.

She walked quickly and switched on all the lights in the kitchen. The sound stopped. After a few seconds, it started again. She knew where it was coming from. *Back door.* The sound grew louder.

She gasped when the backyard door was forced open. A bald guy with a gray mustache stood tall on the aluminum rail with a gun in his hand. His right leg pushed the glass door further. He looked her up and down with a disgusting smile.

She felt the chill in her spine. "Who are you? Go away,

or I'll call the cops."

"Oh dear! You know me very well!"

"What? Just go away. I swear to God I will kill you if you come closer." Her hands trembled. Blood pumped up in her face and made it very warm.

"Kill me? How are you going to do that? With your bare hands, Maria?"

The bald guy smiled and showed his ugly yellow teeth.

How does he know my name?

He moved forward with the gun pointed directly at her head. He smelled really, really bad, as if he had not taken a shower for weeks, if not months. He inched forward and said, "Oh, my dear Maria! You are going to live with me happily forever! Did you forget all those sweet words you chatted with me just a few minutes ago?" He laughed out loud.

"Huh?" Her eyes widened. *This guy is Justin?*

She screamed, "Help! Someone help please!"

The guy snorted and slapped the Colt pistol frame sideways to her head. She fainted in a second.

Jay Sanchez took a deep breath and looked around. He had been watching Maria and Shannon for the last week since he spotted Maria in a Forever 21 store. He had a thing for Hispanic girls. It did not take much effort for him to get to know Maria.

A fake account on Facebook and a cute boy's picture downloaded from a European social networking site did the trick. The girl fell for it just like butter on a flame and spelled out details about when she would be alone in the house. The backyard door was a joke. All it took was a metal cutter and a couple of strong pushes. The absence of a security system made his job easier.

Jay grabbed Maria and put her on the shoulder of his big frame. He switched off all the lights. He slowly walked around and made sure there was no one else in the house. He shoved the gun down in his jacket as he came out of the house.

He scanned the narrow street. There were no lights. It was dark, just the way he wanted.

He replayed the route he would need to take as he walked toward his vehicle, which was parked on the street. He would be on San Mateo Drive in three minutes. Then, it would take another twenty minutes to reach his house in the hills. The girl was heavier than he expected. He took long strides to reach the vehicle before opening the trunk of the Subaru and throwing the girl inside. She was still unconscious. He wrapped her mouth and hands with duct tape and closed the trunk lid.

He looked at the street and the girl's house one more time. He just realized that it was not much of a thrill. If there had been some resistance and a little fight, it would have been meaningful, he thought. He made a mental note for himself to raise the bar the next time.

He opened the driver-side door and lowered himself into the seat. The clock on the dashboard displayed 9:15 p.m.

"In and out in fifteen minutes, not bad! I should aim for ten minutes next time!" he said to himself with pride.

He calculated it would take about thirty minutes to reach

his house. The girl should be awake by then. Duct tape would take care of her in the meantime. It would take some time for her to understand what was going on. Before that happened, she would be in his house.

He stretched his legs and hands. *Good job, Jay boy!* His hands touched the cushioned interior of the roof.

Just then, he felt something on his neck.

A long steel wire was wrapped around his neck and pulled him down backward. Jay sensed the danger, quickly brought down his outstretched hands, and aimed a strong punch at the person in the back. Whoever was hiding behind him knew what he was doing. Jay's punch went nowhere. The guy behind the seat ducked his head without losing his grip on the garrote. Jay tried again, but his hands were throwing punches in the air. He struggled to breathe. The guy in the back twisted the wire harder, using his right arm while holding his left arm steady. The pain was excruciating. Jay stopped throwing punches and used his hands to try to pull the wire out. It was too late already. Steel wire cut the right side of his neck. Jay felt blood on his hands because of the pressure he applied to the wire. He pushed his head backward to loosen the wire. The headrest stopped him. Just then, the wire was tightened and twisted a little more. Jay started kicking his legs, which were blocked by the base of the steering wheel. About ten seconds later, he died.

The guy sitting in the backseat did not let the wire go. He held his position for one more minute. He grabbed Jay's right hand, pulled it backward, and checked the pulse. No pulse. He let the wire go, jumped to the passenger seat like a trained monkey, and stared at Jay, whose body emitted a combo smell of vodka and Heineken.

He removed a phone from Jay's pants. Then, he attached

the voice changer to it and dialed 911. He waited for a few seconds and then provided the location of the dead man to the operator.

Before jumping out of the van, he took a black marker from his backpack and started writing on the dead man's face.

Chapter 7

When Shannon Winters reached the house, she spotted San Mateo Police officers waiting outside. A Sequoia Hospital ambulance, with flashing red lights on the top, was parked across the street. Her vision blurred as she got out of her car and ran toward the front door of the house.

An officer stopped her. "Are you the mother?" he asked as if he were accusing her of something.

"Yes. Where is my daughter? Is she safe? What's going on?"

Before the officer could reply, Shannon started crying.

"Ma'am, please calm down. Your daughter is safe. She's in the ambulance. Let me take you there."

Shannon walked fast with the officer. Maria sat on the EMS chair, behind the ambulance. Her head was wrapped up with a bandage.

"Oh my God. What happened, Maria?" Shannon hugged her tight, and both started crying.

A paramedic, who stood to the side, faced Shannon. "Ma'am, please be gentle. Your daughter was attacked and hit in the head. She seems to be okay, but we need to take her to the hospital to make sure. We'll leave as soon as the cops give us a go."

Shannon nodded and wiped her tears as the officer spoke. "Ms. Winters, my name is Jack Ackerman. I'm a detective with the San Mateo Police. Someone tried to kidnap your daughter. She is in shock. She said someone came through the backyard door and attacked her with a gun."

Shannon gasped.

The officer kept talking. "We got the call around nine thirty. When we came here, we found her in the trunk of that vehicle." He pointed at a Subaru in the distance.

"H–how…?" she stammered. "Did Maria call 911?"

"No. Someone else—Listen…we don't know a lot of things at this point. Just stay with your daughter. I will be back."

Shannon watched the officer walking toward the Subaru and sensed the moisture in her hands. Maria tightly held her hands. Tears flowed from Maria's eyes that were deeply hurt by guilt and terror. "Mom…I am so scared. Don't leave me alone."

"No. I won't." Shannon hugged her tight and sobbed.

∼

Ackerman approached the Subaru. All four doors were left open. Officer Walker stood near the driver-side door.

"Did you find anything interesting, Derek?"

"Nope. Nothing new. I checked three times already.

This guy probably died just before we arrived. The bleeding stopped just now. I checked the guy's—Jay Sanchez—driver license and checked DMV records. He is the owner of the vehicle; he renewed the registration a month ago. He lives, um, never mind—he lived in Belmont Hills if the address on the license is still current. The vehicle looks normal. Well, apart from the dead guy with the warning on his forehead."

Nothing was normal about a crime scene. There was always something. Ackerman knew that he just needed to find it.

He bit the flashlight in his mouth and checked the trunk—bloodstains on the floor mat, possibly from the girl's injury. Other than that, the trunk was clean. He checked the backseat. Heineken beer cases were stacked on one seat. There was nothing on the other seat. He smelled a perfume, could be deodorant. *Sandalwood spray?* He noticed the blood on the headrest of the driver's seat and also on the floor mat behind it. The blood had probably dripped onto the floor. The right side of the dead guy's neck was deeply cut, possibly by a steel wire or a knife. Laceration around the neck. Someone strangled the dead guy from behind with a garrote. *Why?*

Ackerman knelt on the passenger seat and shined the light on Jay Sanchez's forehead. There it was…the familiar face painting.

"Stay away from" was written on the forehead and then, a word on one cheek and another on the other cheek.

"Stay away from little girls."

A bad guy walked into the house. He kidnapped the girl. Then, someone saved the girl, killed the bad guy, and wrote the warning on the dead guy's forehead. *Who is that guy?*

Ackerman sniffed and smelled the deodorant again. It could have been from the killer. Jay Sanchez looked and smelled really bad.

"Well, this is the third time in less than a month. Based on the writing, it could be the same guy who killed the two other kidnappers in the past few weeks." Ackerman paused for a second. "Or…maybe it's a copycat; maybe someone wants to confuse us. The writing is different this time. He is improvising. '*Stay away from little girls*' instead of just '*Stay away*.'"

Walker stared at the dead man and said, "Maybe the bald guy has more real estate on his face!" He smiled at his dry humor. "Whoever killed this guy must be clever."

"Really? He is the *killer* even if he killed the bad guy. I can't believe that you admire the killer."

"Okay, okay…I'm just—never mind. Yeah, you're right. I shouldn't have said that."

Ackerman changed the topic. "We need to impound this vehicle and check it again in daylight. We may find something. Let's go to this guy's house after we are done with the forensic folks."

Chapter 8

At eleven o'clock the next morning, Detectives Ackerman and Walker came out of Shannon's house. Maria was still in shock. *Poor girl will take weeks, if not months, before becoming normal.* Ackerman did not get any new information from Maria. She had narrated the incident for a third time. Her account of Jay Sanchez trolling the Internet for underage girls coincided with what Ackerman had found in Sanchez's house.

Jay Sanchez practically lived on the Internet and had multiple fake accounts in each social media site. Ackerman found no criminal record and nothing in the FBI databases, although Jay had tons of child pornography materials on his laptop, just like other criminal perverts possessed. The guy was a lone wolf, just like a typical kidnapper. *These people do not live and do not let others live either.*

Ackerman leaned on his Ford and looked at the house in front of him before turning his gaze to Walker. "Did you hear from Jay Sanchez's mother?"

Walker shook his head. "Not yet. I left her a message

again today. Hers was the only number in his phone contact list."

"She may not even care if this guy is dead or alive."

Whoever killed Jay Sanchez had planned it, waited for him in the backseat. The killer was organized, patient, and professional. There were no clues except the deodorant smell. Ackerman's mind raced with various questions as he scanned the street. Did the killer know Sanchez was going to kidnap Maria? If so, why did he not stop the kidnapping in the first place? Why did he wait in the backseat for Sanchez to come back? Maybe the killer was an accomplice turned south at the last minute? The *stay away* message could be a distraction.

Ackerman stared at the place where the Subaru had been parked the previous night and wondered what he was missing. His mind stopped racing when he heard Walker's voice. "The girl is terribly shaken. This stupid social media is turning into criminal media."

Ackerman sighed. "Well, some people use technology for good things. Some abuse it." He clicked his tongue and said, "There is always a motive behind each killing. I'm just thinking—maybe the killer is related to the girl."

"What about the girl's father? He might have been involved."

"Girl's parents are divorced. Her father lives in New Jersey. He's on the way."

"What about the boyfriend? Does the girl have one?"

"No. She does not. I talked to her classmates first thing in the morning. Moreover, this killing was not done by a teenager. It was someone professional, someone with a *lot of rage."*

Ackerman's phone rang. He talked for a minute and hung up. "That was the forensic team. Graffiti on Jay Sanchez's face was written by standard permanent markers. There's nothing fancy there. Lab people think that a garrote was used in a strange angle to cut the neck. It was not an amateur job."

"Maybe a hired contract killer?" Walker's brows narrowed.

"None of this makes sense. This is preplanned. Someone waited until Sanchez kidnapped the girl and then killed him and sent the message. I asked computer forensics to check Sanchez's laptop. We may get some clues there." He stopped when he noticed Walker had something to say.

"I listened to the 911 recording a couple of times. It's just like the previous two murders, the one near San Bruno and the one closer to Hillsdale Mall. The caller spoke in a robotic voice. He ended the call with *'Justice is done.'* I'm pretty sure the same guy is involved in all three murders," Walker said in a confident tone.

"You're speculating. The truth is we don't know until we catch the killer." Ackerman sighed. "Chief is talking to the FBI folks as we speak. They have more resources and better technology. They may be able to find the killer."

"I really hope so."

Chapter 9
Claudia Turner, January 22

Claudia Turner smiled back at the cashier who said, "Try another card; that may work!" She nodded, pulled out another credit card from the wallet, and swiped it. "Declined." Claudia sighed before trying the same card two more times.

A young man with tattoo-covered biceps, standing right behind her, threw his hands up in the air. He looked at the cashier and said, "It's nine o'clock on Friday night. But you keep only one counter open. *And* your payment terminal won't behave. Look at all these people waiting in the line." His long silver earrings were dancing, along with his head.

Someone behind suggested, "This is why I carry cash all the time. Cash is king!"

"Come on, Mommy! I'm hungry! I want to open that box!" Emily looked over her right shoulder and pointed to the box of chocolate candy in the cart.

Claudia ignored Emily, who sat on the cart seat and gave an apologetic look to the cashier. "Let me try one more time.

If this doesn't work, I'm going to leave all this stuff here and run to the ATM and come back." She swiped and waited for the damned thing to get approved.

Approved.

"Thank God!" She exhaled. "*Now*, we can go." She finally smiled at Emily and pushed the cart to the parking lot.

"What happened, Mommy? You don't have money?"

"I have money! Their machine is old. It's not reading the card."

Emily giggled. "How can the machine read, Mommy?"

"You'll be surprised when you realize what all these machines do!" Claudia smiled as she took Emily from the cart seat and placed her in the booster seat in the back of the Toyota Prius.

"I don't want to sit in the booster. I want to sit there." Emily pointed to the other corner of the backseat.

"Sure! Once you reach your eighth birthday! Until then, the booster seat will give you a better view!" She kissed Emily on the forehead after buckling her up. "I love you, my little angel!"

"I love you too, Mommy!" Emily waved the tiny teddy bear she was holding in her hand.

Claudia slowly came out of the supermarket parking lot and took a left turn instead of taking the usual right to go to her home in Redwood Shores. She felt embarrassed about not having cash in hand when the credit cards bailed on her. She decided not to enter any store without cash in her wallet. *Always have a plan B.*

A minute later, she took a sharp right to enter the parking

lot in front of the building, the senior center, which was well lit. Then, she drove around the building and parked her car closer to the Foster City Credit Union's ATM terminal, which was right behind the senior center. In contrast to the number of lights in front of the building, there was only one light, just above the ATM machine, in the back of the building. A cereal-bowl-shaped black-colored camera was mounted right next to the light.

Claudia stopped the engine, turned, and looked at Emily. "Mommy will be back in a second. I am going to run to that machine and take the money. Okay?"

"Okay, Mommy! Get some money for my teddy bear too!" Emily giggled.

Claudia laughed as she got out of the car. She looked through the window and waved to Emily before closing the door.

"Hello, young lady," a nasal voice said from behind.

Claudia, rattled a bit, turned around to see an old man, may be seventy years old, on her left. His body was shaking as if he had just come out of a cold shower, in spite of the full-length white fur coat he wore. He adjusted his gray cowboy hat with his trembling hands. "I need your help, young lady! Can you get me some money from that ATM? I have the card, but I can't punch my PIN numbers with these ever shaking stupid hands! Help an old man, young lady." His eyes begged for kindness.

"Gosh, you just freaked me out!" Claudia sighed and moved back a little. "Tell you what; you can try the police station. Just a block away. Go there. The cops will help you out. Me using your ATM card—I don't think that's a good idea."

"That will be great. Sorry for the trouble." He coughed. "Where's that police station again?" The old man's hands were still trembling.

Claudia turned to her right and pointed to a tall building across the street. "That's the library. Behind that—"

The man's hands stopped trembling. He pressed his left thumb on the fingers, moved the hand at a forty-five degree angle, and swiftly punched Claudia in the stomach. His right hand threw a punch to her head, which hit the driver-side door frame. Then, he pushed her into the driver seat, grabbed her hair, and banged her head forcibly on the steering wheel. He moved so quickly that Claudia lost consciousness before she realized what had happened.

He ignored Emily's scream and looked around. He made sure not to look back at the camera. Then, he pulled a white towel from his full fur coat, opened the back door, and pressed the towel to Emily's nose. He removed her from the booster seat and carried her to a black Escalade, which was parked conveniently behind the group of utility meter boxes, diagonally across from the Prius. Then, he gently placed Emily in the backseat, started the engine, and drove toward the Route 92 ramp, which was two minutes away.

Ninety minutes later, FBI Special Agent Theaker arrived in the Foster City Police Station, along with Agents Cooper and Honks from the CARD team.

Child abduction rapid deployment (CARD) teams were formed in October 2005. These teams were designed to deploy teams of experienced personnel to provide on-the-ground investigative assistance to state and local law enforcement. The nationwide CARD team consisted of more than sixty members, with five teams serving each region of the country.

Theaker shook hands with Foster City Police Chief Evans and introduced the FBI team. "Where can we set up our command center?"

Evans pointed to the conference room on the far end. "We have desks set up for you guys. If you need more space, we can set up one in the library next door."

Four minutes later, Evans cleared his throat and started his briefing. "We got a call from a security guard at the senior citizens' center at nine thirty. He found a lady unconscious in the car parked closer to the ATM, which was just behind the senior center. Our officers reached the scene at nine thirty-five. The woman's name is Claudia Turner. She had a severe injury to the head and is being treated in Mills Peninsula Hospital for head trauma. Officers found the empty booster seat in the backseat. Claudia's daughter, Emily Turner, is missing. She's five."

Evans paused for a moment and looked at the team members, who were standing around the table. "Claudia went to the grocery store, two blocks from the ATM location, before going to the ATM. The store receipt shows that she paid at the counter at 9:02. We checked with the cashier. There was only one cashier in the store. She confirmed that Claudia and her daughter were in the store at that time. Assuming that Claudia came out of the store around 9:03, she should have reached the ATM terminal around 9:10. The senior center's security guard spotted the car at 9:30. Something happened in those twenty minutes. Someone took the child." He exhaled.

"I would start with the security guard. Nothing would have happened without him knowing about it. He may be involved in this," Theaker said.

"He's the security guard for the senior center. He's supposed to patrol the area around the center every thirty minutes. The ATM is located in the back of the building, in a corner. The guard is very much on our suspect list. He swears that he did not hear any scream for help. Right now, the only person who can tell us what happened there is Claudia. She is still unconscious. We contacted her husband. He was in an offsite meeting in Novato. He's on the way to the hospital. He said that Claudia called him around eight o'clock on the way to the store. We'll get a better picture of what happened when Claudia is ready to talk."

"There must be cameras near the ATM," Cooper said.

"Yes, there were two, one above the ATM, one on the ATM itself. We already reached out to the bank people. They're working on getting the camera feed to us."

Honks said, "We need to check out the crime scene. A camera mounted in the ATM itself won't be very useful. Its coverage is limited. Our best bet is the other camera on top of the terminal. Hopefully, it captured what happened."

"Do we have pictures of the girl?" Theaker asked.

"Yes, we got them from the father. The man is devastated. We issued an Amber Alert just before you guys walked in," Chief Evans said.

Theaker rubbed his temple. "We should take a look at the crime scene."

"Sure, it's just a block away."

∽

Agent Cooper opened the driver side door of the Toyota Prius and inspected the interior while Honks looked around and stared at the camera mounted above the ATM.

"This should have good coverage, from here to there." Honks moved his arms in a V-shape. "This must have covered what happened in that car."

Cooper nodded and opened the right back door of the vehicle. On other end of the backseat, there was an empty booster seat. Mild smell of a chemical, possibly chloroform. No sign of a struggle in the backseat. A small teddy bear with a tiny pink hat was thrown upside down on the floor mat.

Cooper opened the trunk to find two bags of groceries and a box of chocolate candy. The trunk organizer was neatly arranged in the far right of the trunk. He opened the trunk tool box and checked if anything was missing. He was expecting to find a bloodstained wrench or jack. Nothing. The tools were neatly arranged as if never touched.

Cooper came out of the car and surveyed the area. The ATM terminal was located right behind the senior center. There was only one light, just above the ATM. Lights behind the center were switched off to conserve energy after the center was closed at nine o'clock.

On his right was the back of the senior center. To his left was a pitch-black empty lot. Straight ahead, he faced a small trail adjacent to Foster City Lake. He walked closer to the trail and directed his gaze at two men playing guitar near the lake's shore, under the structure that resembled a Chinese hat.

He turned around and faced Honks. "This is not a remote place. There are people around. It's Friday night, for God's sake. I can understand why the woman didn't have second thoughts about coming to this ATM location." He thought for a second. "How about the cameras in the front of the building?"

"I just checked. There's no camera in the senior center. They didn't think it was necessary. There were only two cameras, both near the ATM," Honks said.

Cooper stopped what he was about to say when he spotted Theaker, who was standing next to a black Chevy, which was parked ten feet from the Prius, signaling him to come over.

Theaker said in a louder voice, "We got the video feed," as he placed a silver-colored HP laptop on top of the Chevy's trunk. His left hand was holding the mobile phone while his right hand operated the laptop.

"Okay, I'm in. What should I click now?" Theaker waited impatiently for the answer from the person at the other end of the call.

He spent the next three minutes navigating around the bank's compliance website before being able to see the video feed. Agents Cooper and Honks took each side of Theaker and stared at the empty parking lot in the video shown on the laptop screen.

The top right of the video indicated 9:08 p.m. when a Toyota Prius pulled up close to the curb. The woman in the driver's seat turned around and talked to someone in the backseat. Then, she got out, smiling and waving. *There—*

A tall man wearing a cowboy hat talked to the woman, who looked frightened. The man was facing away from the camera. His face below his eyes was visible. He had a long face and wrinkled skin. His forehead, eyes, and ears were hidden by the large cowboy hat. He said something to the woman. Then, he attacked her before pushing her into the car.

"Freeze there," Honks said hurriedly.

Theaker stopped and looked at the frame. The man's face was still not visible. He cocked his head sideways to expose just the top of his hat.

Honks looked disappointed, compressed his lips, and watched the rest of the video feed after Theaker clicked the play button.

The man pulled the sun visor down using his left hand without looking away from the woman, before banging her head on the steering wheel. He acted very casually, as if he did such head-banging on a regular basis.

"The bastard planned this," Honks murmured as he watched the man in the video opening the backdoor and lifting the girl out of the car.

Chapter 10

Tracy Zhang, February 20

Harrison logged onto the website and noticed seventy new posts in the last twenty-four hours. That was a lot for a day. He had been a regular visitor to underground Internet forums since the day he returned to the United States. If anyone had any doubts about human evolution, they should pay a visit to one of these shady websites. It was pretty much impossible to spot anyone with basic human decency.

He started reading new posts one by one. Someone from Cambodia offered human kidneys for sale. Some guys asked for partners to trade drugs. When Harrison looked at the next post, he stopped and stared at it. It was written by a guy who went by the username funSeventeen. He asked whether vodka could be mixed with Gatorade and if the mixture could give away the smell. It was obvious from the tone of the post that the guy was not just planning to drink Gatorade with vodka; he also wanted to give it cunningly to someone, possibly an innocent girl. Harrison posted a convincing reply. Then, he sent a private message to funSeventeen with the offer to help if he had more questions.

The bait worked, funSeventeen replied in less than a minute. "Thanks, bro. It should be fun. We have a party tonight. Will have fun with school nerd. Asian chick!"

"Cool. Keep vodka-to-Gatorade ratio, one to three. I can supply vodka to you," Harrison replied, hoping that he would get a chance to meet with funSeventeen.

"No, man. we have it already, lots of it :-)" The message came back at lightning speed.

He sighed and sent out a reply. "Okay. Have fun!" Then, he checked all the other posts by funSeventeen. Some of the posts were about having sex with the teacher in a school bathroom. Some were about his adventure in Big Basin Redwoods State Park, which was closer to the San Jose area. Then, he noticed funSeventeen's avatar, which was the image of a T-shirt. There was some picture on the shirt, but he couldn't make out what it was. The website's avatars were mostly sixteen-by-sixteen icons. It was hard to make sense of that small space. He downloaded the avatar and used open-source software to magnify the image without losing the quality.

The avatar appeared to be a school mascot. But there was no school name on it.

Now, he had to find the school. He started with private high schools in the San Jose area. There was no match for the logo. He checked the websites of all public high schools in the San Jose School District. Then, he found it.

～

Tracy Zhang was a little excited and a lot anxious. She could not believe when Dave, the coolest guy in the school, asked her to come to the party. She was totally clueless about what had attracted him to her. She was a resident geek, not a striking beauty. When she enrolled in Bay Creek High School two years ago as a freshman, she had a panic attack. She had wanted to stay in middle school forever and did not have the confidence to survive high school. However, two years flew by.

During her junior year in high school, she wrote a research paper about the Internet of Things when her classmates were trying to figure out how Internet communication protocols worked. The research paper won the science competition at San Jose State University. The school principal was very proud and put her picture on the notice board with the slogan "Resident geek of Bay Creek!"

Until that point, Tracy had had few friends. When the new title "resident geek" came along, those friends also disappeared.

When Dave showed up in her physics lab one day and congratulated Tracy, she was speechless for a few seconds. "I'm sorry. What is this about?"

Dave seemed to enjoy her innocence. "Oh, you are so modest! The entire school knows you won the science competition!"

"Oh, that…It was last month! It's no biggie."

"Hmm, maybe for you. But for the rest of us, it's a big deal! I wish I could be like you." Dave shook her hand.

Tracy was mesmerized. She had replayed that moment in her mind thousands of times since then.

Although she was not a fan of any sports, she started following football so she could have a meaningful conversation with Dave if he ever came around. He did come around a few times but never discussed football. He kept on talking about how brilliant she was, which was pretty boring.

Last Wednesday, he stopped her in the hallway when she was rushing toward the lab. "Hey, Tracy! We're having a party on Saturday night. Can you come?" Before Tracy could say a word, Dave put his palms together and said, "Don't say no! Please!"

It was the first time in her life someone had invited her to a party. On top of it, the school's heartthrob had almost begged. Tracy felt the butterflies in her stomach as she smiled and said, "Yes!"

~

Tracy adjusted her hair to hide the big forehead she had inherited from her father. Then, she adjusted the rim of her glasses and looked at the GPS screen mounted on the car dashboard. "Mom, we're almost there."

"Are you sure this boy gave you the correct address? I do not see any party house!"

"They don't put a sign in front of the house, Mom! Turn right; I know that boy." She was totally excited. As soon as they turned right, they saw the house with the school crowd on the front porch. She spotted a girl from the senior class. "Mom, this is the house!"

Jennifer Zhang stopped the car at the curb. "I think I should wait here. I am not going to do anything at home. I have the Kindle with me. I will be reading until you come back." She did not want to leave her alone.

Tracy leaned forward, hugged her, and smiled. "You are

so sweet, Mom! I don't know how long the party is going to last. I don't want Dave to think I'm a little child or something, you know. I want to act like a grownup. If you stay here, the guys are going to notice. It'll be embarrassing!" She pointed at the cars leaving the house. "See, every other parent is just dropping off. No one stays here, Mom."

Jennifer Zhang sighed. "I never thought I would let you go to a party at this age. Be safe…"

"I'll be fine, Mom. Don't worry!" Tracy jumped out of the car and waved as she made her way into the crowd. She was a little scared and a lot excited. This was her first party ever. Her eyes eagerly looked for Dave, but there was no sign of him.

She spotted some girls she knew from the school and nervously greeted them. They basically ignored her. She looked around the house. There was still no sign of Dave. She started wondering if she had entered the wrong house. *Oh God, that would be embarrassing.*

Someone touched Tracy's shoulder from behind. "Hey, Tracy! Thanks for coming." Dave seemed surprised.

"Thanks for inviting me." She thought it was lame immediately after saying it. "Cool party. You have a beautiful house."

"Thanks. My folks are out of town. That's another reason to throw a party!" He appeared a little drunk as he laughed out loud.

Tracy wanted to ask when the party would end. It was different from what she had imagined.

"Do you want a drink?" he asked.

"No! I'm not supposed to drink. My mom will kill me!"

"Oh, Crazy Tracy, I was asking about soda and such. There's also a lot of food there in the kitchen. Come on." He held on to her hand as he walked toward the kitchen. She wanted to hold on to his hand forever.

The kitchen was huge. It was bigger than her living room. Her mom would have cried in joy if she had seen the size of that kitchen. Pizza boxes were scattered all over the place, along with soda cans and cookies. A big box of chocolates was sitting on the middle of the island. *Chocolates!*

"Take whatever you need. I need to run now, but I'll be back. Lots of people here know you. Socialize! Don't be shy." Dave quickly turned around and ran toward the living room.

Lots of people know me? That's strange. Tracy took a plate, gathered a lot of chocolates, and grabbed a Diet Pepsi. She looked around the kitchen until she got bored and then walked into the living room. She saw a boy running around without a shirt. Two boys screamed in the backyard. *Weird.*

A long, dark-blue couch was moved from the center to the far-right corner of the living room. Some boys were busy setting up the stereo system in the far left corner. By the size of the speakers, she realized that she would need to tolerate lots of decibels. *How do they even get these things in the car?*

Tracy walked around for a few minutes and then went into the backyard, which was huge as well. There was a long wooden table in the left corner on which beer bottles were stacked and lots of bags of potato chip. A few guys danced without any music.

She looked at the cloudy sky and wondered what her mother was doing. *Probably worrying.*

"There you are!" She turned around after hearing the

voice from behind. Dave ran his hands through his hair and smiled like Prince Charming. "I was looking for you in the living room. What are you doing here?"

"Nothing. Just looking around."

"Come on; let's go to that table." He pointed to the small table in the far right corner. "I just brought Gatorade for you. Let's see who finishes the bottle first!" He laughed as he lifted two bottles. She wanted to keep looking at his smile.

"Gatorade drinking contest? That sounds lame!" She winked.

"Okay then, how about a beer contest?"

"Hell, no. I'll take Gatorade!" She shook her head and laughed.

"There you go. Let's do it!"

Dave gulped the entire bottle of Gatorade while Tracy finished only half. "Looks like you lost! Do you want to try again?"

"I had some soda already. I feel full."

"Come on; don't give up!" He winked, quickly walked to the table in the left corner, and brought two more Gatorade bottles. "Okay, let's try these on the count of three!"

She finished the bottle in two gulps. It didn't taste like Gatorade.

"Wow! You did it. Way to go!" he shouted behind a blurry white screen.

She felt the burning sensation in her stomach. "I don't feel very good. My stomach hurts." She burped.

"Oops, come on. I'll take you to the washroom upstairs."

He grabbed her hand and led the way. The stairs were wobbly and slippery. She promised herself not to get into any more stupid drinking contests. *What was I thinking?*

He turned right after reaching the second level and ushered her into the large bedroom. "This is my parents' bedroom. Bathroom is in that corner. Take it easy. I'll run downstairs and see if I can find any medicine in the kitchen."

She felt warm as she walked toward the bathroom door and then stopped. Her head hurt. She sat cross-legged on the king-size bed, which faced the window, and stared at the full moon. She caught a glimpse of a shadow near the bathroom door. She wanted to check it out, but her legs were numb. She placed a pillow on her lap and clutched it with both hands to soothe her trembling stomach. When she closed her eyes, she felt like she was floating in the air.

Chapter 11

When Dave came back to the bedroom, Dima and Ray came along. "Check this out!" Dave threw his hands up and started making movements, which resembled a folk dance from the early fifteenth century. "She's already crashed! Man, just two bottles! Man, just two!" He took his iPhone and checked the battery to make sure he had enough juice to take pictures—maybe a couple of videos.

Dima locked the door. "Today is our lucky day, man. I never did an Asian chick!"

"Her mother is Chinese. Father is Korean. It's multicultural man!" Ray giggled.

Dima and Ray dragged Tracy gently from the corner of the bed and placed her in the middle. Dima lay down on one side of her. Ray took the other side and removed her glasses. Both got ready to undress her.

Dave looked at them and winked. "Guys, do your thing. You're in a movie, folks!"

Dima laughed like a hyena and showed his smoke-stained

yellow teeth. He looked at Ray and said, "Since eighth grade, Dave has wanted to direct a porn movie. Can you believe that?"

Ray didn't reply. He looked confused and stared at the white wall adjacent to the bathroom door.

Dave stopped smiling and followed Ray's eye movement. Just then, he felt like someone had put his head inside a bonfire. "Fuck…" He dropped the phone, put both his hands on his head, and knelt down on the floor. Someone grabbed his neck, pulled him up, and threw an elbow strike to the center of his head. He wasn't sure if someone had attacked him or if the vodka was doing its magic. He fell on his face on the hardwood floor and tasted varnish.

～

Harrison looked straight at the people on the bed. He wasn't sure if the girl was half-awake. The boy on her right jumped off the bed. He was six-foot-two, well-built, and looked like a quarterback.

"Who the hell are you? Who let you in here?" Ray started shouting as he moved forward. He looked at Dave, who was flat on the floor, with disgust and fear.

Harrison twisted his neck, generating a bone-cracking sound, and stared at Ray without saying a word.

"You're in big trouble, asshole." Infuriated, Ray threw a punch at Harrison, who quickly moved to his left and let Ray's hand pass by the right side of his face. Then, Harrison threw a hard punch with his palm. The punch landed right below Ray's bottom teeth. Ray felt the blood on his lips.

Now, Harrison threw his right elbow with full force at Ray's head, which was the final blow in Ray's life.

Harrison pulled a knife from under the robe and slid it through Ray's neck. Lifeless, Ray fell down like a slaughtered sheep.

It took a few seconds to sink in for Dima. He had been close friends with Dave since kindergarten. When the principal had decorated the school notice board with Tracy's picture, he provoked Dave. "Lot of girls may fall for you, but not this one. She's too nerdy for you!"

Dave took that as a challenge and took baby steps to gain her trust and make her come to the party. Just like they planned, she was drunk and was only a few inches away from him but still not touchable.

"Who are you, man? Get the hell out of here. There's no money here." Dima wasn't sure whether that was the smart thing to say. He was too nervous to think of anything meaningful. He just wanted to open the door and run. When he saw the monk in a red robe walking toward him with a gun, he could not control it. He peed in his pants.

Chapter 12

San Jose Police Detective Wong scanned the room one more time. Two guys on the floor, one guy on the bed. Two had been shot in the head, and one died from a knife wound to the neck. The killer took time to write something on each victim's forehead.

STAY AWAY

FROM

LITTLE GIRLS

There were multiple shoeprints on the floor. It was going to take some time to sort out which ones belonged to the killer. The killer could have entered from the balcony or from the front door. There was no one alive in the room to talk about it.

He looked at Detective Montgomery, who was taking notes on a small scratch pad with a blue Pilot pen. "There were similar murders in the Bay Area. Girls were abducted and sedated. All kidnappers get killed eventually. Killer seems to have focused his gun on their private parts. Weird. Same warning is written on all the dead guys. There's a pattern here. It's obvious that we have one butcher out there slaughtering all these guys. I just don't understand how the killer knows so much about kidnappers before we do." Wong sighed.

"*This girl...*" Montgomery pointed at the empty bed as if Tracy were still there. "The girl was not kidnapped. All these kids came here for a party. There was a 911 call from one of these guys. When we came in here, it was a total mess," he said.

"Did anyone speak on that call?"

"Yes. Someone spoke in a robotic voice as per the operator, giving the address of this house."

"Whose house is it?"

"Millers. Big shot in real estate. His wife is a former fashion model. They're out of town." Montgomery pointed at Dave, who lay dead in the pool of blood. "Their only son arranged this party. I doubt if the parents know about it."

"911 call came from his phone?"

"Yes, sir. The guy had the phone attached to his ear." Montgomery pointed at the iPhone lying next to Dave's dead ear.

Wong pulled the gloves through his fingers and scrolled through the call log. There was a 911 call at 7:15 p.m. and another call, which lasted for a minute at 6:55 p.m. He dialed that number and put the phone on speaker mode. A rap music ringtone came from the king-size mattress, through the dead guy's jeans pocket.

"Hmm, killer did his job between 6:56 and 7:15." Wong touched the camera icon and touched the album icon. When he saw the first picture that came up, he muttered, "Oh shit."

The boys were trying to rape the girl and had filmed it. Could there be any video? Wong clicked the home screen button and played all the videos. There were two videos. The first video was filmed at five o'clock in the evening. There was nothing other than boys smirking and laughing for no reason. The second video was filmed at five minutes past seven. Two of the boys posed obscenely next to the girl on the bed. The boys talked. Then, the video screen showed the shaky wall and the ceiling. Strong thud. Then, the screen went dark.

"Too bad it didn't catch the killer's face or the voice," Montgomery said.

"He was careful not to say a word." Wong looked around and rubbed his temple. "There's no blood trail. When victims are stabbed and killed, usually there would be a blood trail." He immersed himself in thoughts about what could have happened before asking, "Who's the girl? Did you check?"

"The girl is a junior at Bay Creek. All these kids are from the same school."

"Let's talk to these kids. The phone pictures are disturbing. These boys did something. We need to figure it out."

Wong and Montgomery walked down the stairs to face the group of forty boys and girls sitting on the living room floor. Three girls, sitting together on the red couch placed closer to the wall, sobbed.

"Guys, can anyone tell me what this party is about?" Wong looked at the crowd.

A boy with orange-dyed hair raised his hand. "Dave threw the party. His team won the football championship."

"Are you guys all in the same school? Same class?"

"Yeah, same school," the boy said.

A girl leaning against the wall said, "But—not the same class. There was a junior. Rest of us are seniors."

"The girl who was taken in an ambulance is a junior? What is her name?" Wong asked.

"Tracy. She's a nerd. I don't think she was *even invited*," a blond girl growled. She sat on one arm of the long leather couch placed adjacent to large speakers, which were no longer pumping out loud music. She placed her left leg firmly on the couch and left her other leg bouncing uncomfortably over the side.

A boy with a thin mustache stood up. "Dave invited her. That's what she told me when she walked into the house. I saw Dave take her upstairs."

"No shit!" the blond girl growled again.

Wong turned to Montgomery. "Please get everyone's name and address. We may get some prints from the phone. Or not. We will try anyway." Then, he looked at the blond girl, who was staring at him with her blue eyes. "Did you see anyone suspicious going up there?" He raised his left hand toward the stairs.

The blonde snorted. "I think everyone here is a suspect." She looked away.

Chapter 13

Samantha waited for the class to end. She had office hours with Professor Mitchell immediately afterward. The teaching assistant spoke in a croaky voice. "Make sure you understand how the interest rates work. Otherwise, you'll fail miserably in all internship interviews." She ignored the subtle threat and drew a mind map in her notebook.

> Class ends at noon. It would take three minutes to reach Prof. Mitchell's office. Ten minutes to wait in the line, 12:13 to 12:33, Prof. Mitchell a.k.a. Prof. Yell! Another seven minutes to walk to cafeteria. 12:40. Review notes, then walk to George Hall for Midterm at 1:00.

The wait wasn't so bad in Professor Mitchell's office. Samantha sat on the wooden chair with wobbly legs, after greeting the professor. "I have a question about the term paper."

"Okay. Shoot!"

"You asked us to go back in time and look at unsolved

crimes. I want to write something about one of the current unsolved crimes. I want to write about the killer who kills all the bad guys."

"Which killer are you talking about? There are so many of them."

Samantha noticed the frustration in the professor's voice.

She pulled a few sheets from her backpack and spread them on the desk. "These were all in the news. You know, the guy who wrote the warnings on dead bodies?"

"Stay away from little girls?" Professor Mitchell nodded. "I know. That's an interesting case. I never came across a murderer who took time to write warnings for dead people! The guy's already dead; why write the warning?" He looked up to see if Samantha would smile at his joke.

She forced a smile. "Actually, the warning is not for the dead guy. The warning is for people who would attempt such a thing." She continued, "It's not just one case. There were a couple of cases with the same pattern." She pulled a printout of a US map before the professor raised his hand and stopped her.

"What exactly do you want to do? Do you want to write about this killer?"

"Yes. Here's the thing. I want to focus on the motivation of the killer. My gut feeling is that the killer is a good guy."

Professor Mitchell smirked. "How can the *killer* be a good guy?"

"Well, when someone kills the bad guys, he must be a good guy."

"Not really. The killer may have a beef with the bad guys. Good guys don't kill others. I'm not surprised about your thought process. Fantasy is natural for people of your age."

"What if the good guys get provoked?"

"Hmm, let me ask you this." Professor Mitchell looked straight into Samantha's eyes. "If someone provokes you, would you go and kill that person?"

Samantha shook her head back and forth. "I didn't mean it like that. It's just…you know, there's really something strange with what happened in these killings." Samantha looked quickly at the clock, *12:23*. *Good, right on time.*

Professor Mitchell listened as Samantha narrated her theory.

"Some kind of Robin Hood, that's what you think?" Professor Mitchell looked at the clock, showing his disinterest.

"Not really. Not a Robin Hood. But a guy with a good heart, somehow deeply troubled by the crimes. I want to write about how good people turn into killers."

Professor Mitchell tapped a black Pilot pen on his desk. "Okay. This isn't really what I had in mind when I asked for a paper on criminal behavior. But this could be interesting. I would love to read your paper when it's ready."

Samantha collected the printouts she had spread on the desk and thanked the professor as she got to her feet.

Professor Mitchell nodded with a smile.

She stopped walking toward the door when she heard the professor's voice from behind. "You know what? One of my students is a special agent in the San Francisco FBI office. He called me to inquire about you!"

He waved his right hand to calm her down after seeing

the confusion in her face. "Nothing to worry about! You applied for an FBI internship, right? That's why he called me. I told him good things about you." He smiled warmly.

Samantha's face lit up. "Thank you very much! I have the interview tomorrow in San Francisco."

"Tomorrow? Very good! I hope it goes well. All the best."

Samantha thanked him again and walked out. All of a sudden, the future looked very promising. She stopped outside Kroeber Hall, closed her eyes, and slowly inhaled the breeze coming from the palm trees surrounding Berkeley Art Museum. The air smelled pleasant, and the art museum looked more beautiful than it had the last time she saw it, which was only twenty minutes ago. She pleasantly recalled the conversation she had just had with the professor. Nothing beat the alumni connection when trying to find a job or internship.

Samantha smiled with excitement and walked fast to grab lunch before heading to her midterm exam room. *These exams are so boring.* She could not wait to complete the quarter.

The midterm exam was over by four o'clock. Samantha felt relieved. She briskly walked to the cafeteria adjacent to the campus bookstore, ordered a cinnamon dolce latte, and glanced at the television screen mounted on the wall behind the cashier. A man was crying. His daughter had been kidnapped the previous week and found dead in the morning. *Horrible.* For a parent, there was nothing worse than losing a child. She stared at the picture of the girl. She was only five and looked very beautiful. *What kind of a man would have the heart to kill this girl?* The girl's dead body was found in the woods near the College of San Mateo.

She felt the stiffness in her neck and took a deep breath. *I will join the FBI and save at least one child from these monsters.*

Chapter 14

Samantha Cruz walked briskly to the Berkeley BART station. BART, Bay Area Rapid Transit, was the local subway system, which connected most of the cities in the San Francisco Bay Area. After twenty minutes on the train, she got off at the Civic Center station in San Francisco. She had about thirty minutes to reach the FBI office for the internship interview. She took the escalator to reach the ground level of the train station and started walking toward UN Plaza.

She turned left at Golden Gate Avenue and started walking uphill. Fifteen minutes later, she turned right into Polk Street. On her right, a fifteen-story building stood tall. "FEDERAL BUILDING" was written in big, capital letters, sixty feet above the ground, in the center of the building. Tiny water fountains were pumping water in front of the building. A gentle breeze combined with light drizzle touched her hair. She adjusted her hair and backpack and braced herself for show time.

She opened the giant glass door in the entrance to find

two guards staring at her. One of them said in a monotone. "Put your mobile phone and any metal objects into your backpack, and push it onto the belt. Shoes go in a bin." He pointed to a stack of bins on the right. She did exactly that and waited for the backpack to arrive at the other end of the X-ray machine. She wondered when the security guard had smiled last.

A minute later, she waited in front of the elevator and checked her watch. It was seven minutes before nine o'clock. Right on time. The elevator door opened with a ding. She got in and pressed the number five. As the elevator slowly climbed, she heard her stomach growling in spite of the noisy ride. She gently touched her stomach in an effort to calm it down. The last thing she wanted was to appear nervous.

She got out of the elevator and walked tall to show her confidence until she saw the sign pointing to the FBI field office. The fear crept in again. She dismissed it and briskly walked to her left to find the open door leading to a small waiting room. She expected a receptionist but found none. Portraits of politicians hung on the wall. She observed four chairs and one small glass table, on which crime prevention brochures were spread, in the center of the waiting room.

As she was thinking about how to get the attention of the people inside, she found a small white button next to the door on the wall with a sign in tiny letters: "Press here for assistance." She pressed it, adjusted her hair, and waited.

A few seconds later, a tall man with a dark-blue coat came out. "Samantha?"

"Yes. I'm here for the internship interview." She shook his hand warmly.

"I'm Special Agent Theaker. Come on in." He led the way to the small conference room in the far-right corner. Theaker introduced her to two other people sitting around the conference room table. "This is Assistant Special Agent Jones. This is Agent Rousseau."

Agent Jones was five-foot-ten, handsome, probably Irish. He stood up and shook her hand firmly. Agent Rousseau waved her hand and smiled. Theaker pointed to the chair. "Take your seat. Make yourself comfortable."

Make myself comfortable? He's got to be kidding.

Samantha lowered herself into a small chair in the middle, placed the backpack on the floor, and sat upright. The oval-shaped table showed the wear and tear of twenty years. The three people sitting on the other side of the table looked at each other. Rousseau put her head down and took a serious look at Samantha's résumé on the desk. Theaker gave a silent nod to Jones and looked at Samantha.

"Well, I think we should start." Theaker took five minutes to explain the selection process for interns.

When he had finished his warm-up speech, Rousseau looked up and asked in a stern voice, "Why should we choose you over the other applicants? What makes you so special?"

Samantha looked shocked at the change of tone. She took a second to regain her confidence and said, "Nothing makes me special. I'm sure there are lots of other qualified applicants for the internship. However…" She paused and looked at Jones, who was smiling. "I applied for the internship for only one reason. I want to join the FBI and serve my country. My degree from Berkeley can open the door for good-paying jobs in Silicon Valley. I can take a shot at a start-up and become a millionaire in a few years. But money does not motivate me. I want to serve the country and protect the people, especially young children, from harm. I hope that you will find me a suitable candidate after this interview."

Theaker nodded, took notes, and silently smiled at Rousseau's lousy question. He fired the next question. "How can you protect young children from harm? You can't magically protect them just by joining the FBI. It's not like what you see in the movies! I want to put your expectations in perspective. Remember, a lot of agents die or get injured in the field."

"I understand. I have an inquisitive mind and keep coming up with ideas to catch the bad guys. Having a position inside the FBI would help me to channel my energy and use my intelligence effectively. I could do a lot of amazing things with the resources available in the FBI." She radiated passion and confidence.

"Really? Interesting!" Jones said.

Theaker smiled at Jones and looked at Samantha. "Give us an example. Give us some of your ideas. Let's see if we can use any of those ideas!"

"Sure!" She pulled the backpack from her side and took out a bunch of papers. "This is about the *stay away* killer who saved the children from kidnappers."

She spread the papers on the desk and pointed at the first sheet. "This is the recent case in San Jose. Three high school seniors tried to gang rape a junior after giving her a date-rape drug. Someone came in and killed all three. No one, *no one*, saw the killer who wrote '*Stay away*' all over these guys' faces. The warning is not for the dead guys. It's for pedophiles and bad guys who would attempt such a cruel act."

She moved to the next sheet on the desk. "It's not just one case. There were a couple of cases already with the same pattern. This one happened in Hillsdale Mall a few months ago. Amanda Rivera was kidnapped in broad daylight from the mall parking lot. She was found alive within a few hours. Her kidnapper was brutally murdered."

She pulled out a printout of a US map and ran her fingers over the red dots. "There was a similar case in Thousand Oaks last year. Cardiologist accused of molesting young patients was killed in his clinic. The killer tied up the doctor's staff and made them watch the killing. Later, he asked the nurse to write the warning '*Stay away*' on the doctor's forehead. According to his staff, the killer wore a ski mask. No one saw his face. The doctor's attorney was killed a few days later in Sacramento with the message '*Bad karma*' on his forehead." She caught her breath and continued, "Then, a middle school teacher was killed in Pasadena around the same time. The teacher was accused of molesting his students, but the jury released him after a six-month trial. The teacher was butchered in his home. His right wrist was cut and his hand thrown into the fireplace. When the police reached the dead man's home, they found that the guy was sitting dead on the couch, facing the front door, and holding a small white board with the words '*Stay away from little girls*' on his lap."

"We're aware of those murders, Samantha. Go on." Theaker wanted to know more.

She grabbed a few more sheets from the backpack. "There were three cases in the last week. Just the last week. Two kidnappings and one rape. Five dead people. All these guys are bad guys. They were killed horribly. Warnings were written all over their faces." She spread the pictures of dead guys on the desk. "I strongly believe that the killer is a male in his early thirties. I also believe that he lost a loved one, probably his daughter, recently." She paused for a moment. "These killings are not *revenge* killings. The killings are all over the map on the West Coast. He is possibly a good man spooked by violent crimes. He is frustrated with the judicial system and wanted to take justice into his own hands."

Theaker nodded. "I see. If you were in charge of catching this killer, how would you plan to catch him?"

"I think the first step is to think like him. What would you do if you wanted to catch the pedophiles *before* they did harm to the children? You would go after sex offenders. You would go places these people frequent. The killer is going after bad guys by thinking like them. So, if I think like the killer, I'm sure I'll catch him."

"That sounds like a plan! Why don't you think like the killer and tell us where to find him?" Jones winked.

"Sure! All I need is the desk in this office, access to FBI databases, and some help from forensic and cyber-crime teams. When can I start the job?"

Jones laughed out loud. Theaker and Rousseau smiled at each other.

Chapter 15

Teresa Goldberg, March 4

Quiet hallways suddenly turned into uproarious playgrounds when the bell rang in Belmont Hills Middle School. Teresa Goldberg grabbed her backpack and wrapped it around her right shoulder. Someone touched her shoulder from behind as she pulled the books from under the desk.

"Ready to go? Come on!" Nadia grinned.

Teresa smiled and shook her head. "I have choir practice until six. We're going to sing in Notre Dame Church on Sunday."

Nadia looked a little disappointed. "Okay then. I need to run to catch the bus." She waved and rushed out.

Teresa neatly arranged the books and walked toward the locker located adjacent to the gym.

After shoving the backpack and books inside the locker, she quickly ran to the restroom to splash cold water on her face and gently pressed a wet paper towel on her throat for a minute. *No more squeaky voice.*

She crossed the hall, went downstairs, and turned right to enter the choir room. Ms. Hutchison stood at the entrance of the room and smiled at her. "Hey…you look so bright today, even after one full crazy day!"

She blushed. "Thank you, Ms. Hutchison."

"Ready for some fun? Let's rock!" She watched Ms. Hutchison's slim body shaking like Lady Gaga's. Poor Ms. Hutchison was no match for Lady Gaga, especially in the weight department. She had lost most of her excess weight since she was forced to eat gluten-free, lactose-free food.

She noticed more people than usual in the room. "Okay. Let's start with 'Follow Peace'!" Ms. Hutchison said as she walked toward the center of the room. Then, she ordered everyone to stand in their designated places and started conducting.

It was ten minutes past six in the evening when the choir practice was over. Teresa felt hungry. But she didn't want to miss the bus. Otherwise, she would have to wait for another hour to catch the next one. She ran upstairs to the locker room, grabbed the backpack, and quickly walked to the bus stop.

The bus, displaying "260 San Carlos Caltrain" in big, bold digital letters, came right on time. *My lucky day.*

She climbed up, waved her student pass, and looked around. An elderly woman was sitting just behind the driver. No one else was in the bus. She took the first seat on the left and grabbed her phone from the backpack's front pouch. Her school had the strict policy of keeping mobile phones switched off while on campus. She switched on the phone and fired away a text message: "Mom, I'm on 260. Will be there in 20."

The bus made five stops and stopped at the corner of Carlmont Drive and Lyall Avenue, a few feet away from the entrance of the water dog lake park. The park was popular among area residents who loved the park dedicated to dogs. Occasionally, mountain lions also visited the trail. Belmont City put up a big sign to warn the residents about mountain lions and inform them of what to do if they happened to encounter one face-to-face.

Teresa waved to the driver and jumped off the bus. She turned to her right and started walking uphill. The street was almost dark except for a light at the corner of the street. A cool breeze blew through the *Juniperus californica* trees lined up on the left side and gently touched her face. Her family lived in an apartment one block away from the bus stop, right next to the corner of Lyall and Continental. She looked around to see if anyone was around. No one. Cars were lined up on her right.

She slowly walked on the pedestrian path, between *Juniperus* trees and the long line of cars, and narrowly avoided the dog poop on the pathway. She looked down, walked slowly, and carefully avoided a few more dog poop piles.

Her phone beeped. She stopped walking and looked at the message. Nadia had sent a text. "Do you want to go to the mall tomorrow?" Teresa smiled and shook her head. Nadia loved to roam around the mall every weekend. As Teresa resumed walking and started typing the reply, she heard a rustling sound coming from behind the trees on her left. She stopped.

No more rustling.

She continued her typing. "I'll call you tomorrow. Lots of homework!" She hit the send button, avoided one more dog poop pile, and looked up a little.

Just then, a man quickly came from behind the bulky tree on the left. He was a tall, ugly old man with a disgusting grin.

A chill went down her spine. She moved to her right to avoid the man but lost her balance, placed her right shoe on the edge of the pedestrian walk, and fell on the road on her right, between two cars.

"Oh my! Sorry, I scared you. Let me help you." The man extended his left arm, which was brown, wrinkled, and hairy. She sat on the road, looked up, and shook her head in panic.

"Don't worry. I like helping good girls!" He shoved his right hand inside his jacket and took a white towel out. "This will help you to forget the pain."

As Teresa tried to get up, the man quickly put his left arm around her head, placed the white towel over her face, and pressed it against her nose. In a second, her nostrils tickled cold and her head hurt. The man smiled like Count Olaf.

∿

The man looked around. No one was in the vicinity. He lifted Teresa, who was unconscious and leaned on his shoulder; walked backward, and chirped his remote to open the Cadillac Escalade parked conveniently close to where she fell. He kicked his foot under the bumper to open the power-lift gate to open the trunk door. He gently laid her inside and quickly closed the door. He scanned the street one more time and then jumped into the driver's seat and started the engine. He drove down Lyall Avenue for a few seconds, took a quick U-turn to climb back up the same street, and stopped at the stop sign at the corner of Lyall and Continental. As he watched for oncoming traffic from the left, he noticed a Hispanic woman walking down the footpath on Lyall. He rapidly turned right onto Continental. The Escalade's tires squealed loudly.

The woman was rattled by the squealing and turned to her left to see the speeding vehicle. She pinched her nose to avoid smelling the vehicle's exhaust as she continued to walk down Lyall. Her eyes scanned for Teresa.

~

Bob McFarlane played drum on the steering wheel as he waited for the traffic signal on Ralston Avenue. It felt good to grab the girl. He wondered how Thomas would react when he got to see her.

After driving on Ralston Avenue for seven minutes, he took the Route 280 South exit toward Half Moon Bay. He opened the window and enjoyed the refreshing wind flowing from Crystal Springs. He desperately wanted to floor the pedal to reach his destination quickly. But he controlled his enthusiasm. The last thing he needed now was to get stopped by a cop for speeding.

He drove steadily at sixty miles an hour and then took the exit leading to Route 84. Then, he drove for another twenty minutes and took the Alpine Road exit. Here, he took a sharp right and drove on rough road for seven minutes. He passed a cattle farm on the right and stopped in front of a large house. He got out of the Escalade, stretched his arms, and then whistled. Two pit bulls stormed out of the house and surrounded Bob. He sat on his knees and hugged both dogs.

"Hello, boys! Ready for a treat?"

The dogs howled with excitement.

He scanned the surroundings before lifting the trunk

door. The girl was still unconscious. *Barbie Doll.* He lifted her, placed her head on his left shoulder, and carried her inside the house. The pit bulls followed him.

∿

Belmont Police Detective King consoled Gabriella Goldberg. "Please calm down. We're here to help you. Can you please describe what happened?"

Gabriella wiped her tears. "Teresa sent me a message at six twenty. She was on the bus. She normally walks on her own. Today, I went to the bus stop to pick her up because it was dark already. I was just a minute late," she bawled.

The detective gently touched her shoulder. "Ma'am, then what happened?"

"I couldn't find Teresa. But…" She pointed at the violet-colored backpack lying on the floor and cried. "Her school bag was lying on the pedestrian walk. I called her." She took a deep breath before she continued, "I heard her ringtone. Her phone was abandoned on the road!" she cried from her stomach.

"Did the bus come on time? Did anyone see her getting off of the bus?" the detective questioned.

"I don't know," she sobbed. "Why are you asking me these questions? How come her school bag was lying on the road? Don't you understand?"

"Sorry, Ms. Goldberg. I do understand. I want to make sure."

The detective grabbed the gloves from his coat pocket and pulled them on before inspecting the backpack.

Schoolbooks, notebooks, a pink-colored pencil pouch with Taylor Swift's picture on the top, a calculator, chapstick.

Nothing more.

He looked up and asked, "Do you have pictures of your daughter?"

Gabriella nodded. "I will go and get the pictures." She walked toward the room on the left.

The detective turned to the officer on his right and gave series of instructions. "Call SamTrans and get the bus driver on the phone quickly. The driver will have a fresh memory now. The sooner we talk to the driver, the better…" He paused before adding, "Call the chief and let him issue an Amber Alert now. I'll send the pictures to his phone."

~

Teresa woke up to the barking sound of pit bulls. *The apartment has a no-dogs policy, right, Mom?* Panic surrounded her when she realized that she was not at home. *What is happening? Am I dead?* After three seconds, she remembered the face of the tall, ugly old man and recalled what had happened.

She looked around and could see only pitch-black, except the flickering lights outside the window. Her hands were tied to the chair's armrests, and her legs were tied together with a nylon rope. The rope ended with a knot on one of the legs of the gray couch, which looked very old, on her left. She pushed her legs under the chair in an effort to see if she could break free from the rope but stopped when her heels hurt.

She closed her eyes and took a deep breath. *Is it a bad dream?* She felt like Hermione Granger locked up in a dungeon. She held both armrests tightly, using a firm palm grip, and got up, bringing up the chair along with her body. A little relief formed in her face. She carried the chair by keeping a firm grip on the armrests and slowly walked toward the front door. The rope that tied her legs was long, but not too long. As she took a few steps with the chair on her back, she felt the resistance from the other end of the rope, which was tied to the leg of a monstrous couch. It did not move. One more deep breath and one more pull. She faced the couch and pulled her left leg in an effort to move the couch along. Thud. She lost her balance and fell on the floor along with the chair. The rope around her wrists tightened and triggered pain, which traversed to her biceps.

She bit her lips and controlled herself so as not to scream. Tears flowed down her chin. She composed herself and scanned her surroundings. To her left was a giant-sized leather couch and a wooden door to a room behind the couch. On her right, a big-screen television was mounted on the wall with the surround system below it. She faced the front door, which was closed, possibly locked, and surrounded by arch-shaped windows on both sides. She turned around to see what was behind her—a kitchen, large dining table, and the back door, which was shut.

She slid back into the chair and pushed her knee to the floor. At the same time, she held the firm grip on her chair and pushed to the left. Now, she was back to square one and stared at the flickering lights outside the window. She took a deep breath and prayed.

After a minute, she caught a glimpse of two gray-colored pit bull dogs through the window on her right, mounted three feet away from the front door. The dogs barked and jumped at the same time, trying to catch something. Then, both dogs looked to the right. The tall man slowly walked toward the dogs.

Her heart raced, and panic set in again. *Same guy*. Using all her strength, she lifted the chair and moved to her left.

Then, she moved closer to the couch, creating a small sag in the rope. She moved along the front edge of the couch to stay close to it, to take full advantage of the sag. As she got closer to the window, mounted on the left side of the front door, she screamed at the top of her lungs, "Help! Help me...Somebody help me..."

Seconds later, the front door was violently opened. The pit bulls charged in and came dangerously close to her face. The dogs' eyes looked like flames in the middle of the forest. She screamed, "Go away!"

The man calmed the dogs and looked at the rope that bound her legs together. A smirk formed on his wrinkled face. He spit on the floor.

"You think you're too smart, huh? You have any idea how many times I've done this?" he barked.

Teresa begged. "Please—please let me go. I'm not smart. You are smart. Please let me go."

"What is that noise? *Help! Help!*" he mocked her. "Do you know there is no one around here to help you? You are sitting in an isolated house surrounded by cattle farms and mountains."

He saw the terror in her face and loved it. "Do not worry. We are going to have a good time, okay? Thomas is a good boy; you will like him."

Thomas?

"Please let me go. I won't tell anyone. I'm a good girl. I don't hurt anyone. Okay? Please listen to me." She pleaded with her eyes.

"Okay. I'll listen to you. Go on." He sat down and ran his fingers down the rope attached to the couch.

She looked at him with teary eyes. "My name is Teresa. I am in seventh grade. I am the only daughter of my parents. I volunteer in Belmont library. I am a singer—"

He raised his right hand. "I don't want to hear all this bullshit."

"Please listen. I have a choir performance in Notre Dame Church in two days. I have to practice. It's for God. I sing for God." She paused for a second. "You do believe in God, right? Please let me go. I will pray for you. *Please…*"

He sat cross-legged, raised his chin up, and grinned. "*You* pray for me? Huh!" He shook his head back and forth. "Let me tell you something, little girl. There ain't no God!"

Teresa sniffled. She pushed both palms together and fixed her gaze on him. Her eyes begged for mercy. She remembered the lyrics from the song she had been practicing in choir, "You bind us up when we're broken," and the lyrics gave her strength.

> *You bind us up when we're broken in body and heart;*
>
> *You fill us up when we're empty; Your nature imparts*
>
> *Perfect wisdom and guidance for life's many tests;*
>
> *Perfect comfort and healing and promise of rest,*
>
> *Perfect comfort and healing and promise of rest.*

Chapter 16

Agent Theaker controlled his anger. "Mr. Goldberg, we are doing everything we can to find your daughter. Right now, our entire force is on this case. Please work with us to help you."

Gabriella held her husband's arm tightly and made him sit down. Bill Goldberg looked up and cried, "We moved here because we thought this would be a safe place. We believed in cops taking care of our safety. Our neighborhood is supposed to be safe—" He felt the heavy pain in his chest. Gabriella gently squeezed his hands.

Bill Goldberg took a deep breath, looked at Theaker, and sobbed. "Teresa is my only daughter. Please find her."

Theaker pulled out a chair and sat directly in front of Bill. "Mr. Goldberg, we want to narrow down our focus to find your daughter quickly. Do you have any enemies at work?"

He shook his head. "No. I can't think of any."

"Did you fire anyone recently?"

"No."

"Did any of you notice strange behavior with Teresa's schoolmates, friends in this complex, or anything that struck you as unusual?"

Bill shook his head. His tears continued to run down to his throat. He pulled a napkin from the coffee table and wiped the tears away. "You have to trust me on this. You are wasting time. Teresa wouldn't run away. She is a happy child. She looks forward to every day. She is our reason to live. Her friends are very decent kids. No one gets into trouble. Some sick bastard took our daughter away. Please go and find her instead of asking me all these questions. You have no idea what we are going through."

Theaker fixed his gaze on Bill. "Actually, I do…" He paused before adding, "We have FBI agents and the CARD team working round the clock. We placed a nationwide Amber Alert. Even if the bad guys move to a different state, we will still find them."

He watched Bill sniffling and nodding without saying a word. He gave a silent nod to Detective King, walked out of the living room, and issued a series of instructions to the assistant special agents waiting in the hallway.

∼

Harrison's phone beeped with the Amber Alert at three minutes past eight o'clock. He moved his shopping cart out of the way and checked the text message on his phone. A twelve-year-old girl had been kidnapped in Belmont. His head started hurting badly just like every time he saw the Amber Alert. He abandoned the cart and walked out of the Safeway store, which was located at the corner of Ralston and Alameda. He heard the sirens in the distance.

The sirens grew louder. An ambulance sped through the intersection and took a left on Alameda. Two police cars followed the ambulance in four-second intervals. He rubbed his temple to make the headache go away and failed in that attempt. He ignored the car in the parking lot and decided to take a walk to clear his mind.

He crossed Ralston and took a small street leading to the water dog lake park. The sirens grew louder again. An ambulance zoomed down Carlmont Drive on his left and turned left to reach the apartment complex at the end of the street. Police cars followed.

He took long strides to cross Carlmont Drive and stopped at the entrance to the water dog lake park. He gazed at the FBI agents and Belmont police officers combing the pedestrian path from the park entrance to the end of the street where the ambulance was parked. A minute later, emergency personnel emerged from the corner building and wheeled a middle-aged man into the ambulance. A woman cried and ran behind.

The ambulance left the street with the sirens. Two police officers came out of the corner building. Then, he saw a familiar face. *Joshua Theaker.*

His head hurt like it was going to explode any minute as he struggled to breathe. He slowly walked to his left and sat on the rocky ground near the entrance of the park, just below the sign board warning about the presence of mountain lions in the area. He felt dizzy and closed his eyes. Soon, darkness engulfed him.

Chapter 17

August 2006

As he walked slowly along a narrow path, paved with sharp, tiny stones, Harrison wondered how the guide, walking a few yards ahead of him, was able to walk without any footwear. On his right, a cluster of beautiful peach trees blossomed and gave off a warm and spicy fragrance. Pine trees lined up and decorated the land just above the peach trees. To his left, a breathtaking green valley expanded far into the distance until it hit the Himalayan pine trees in the backdrop of the foothills.

The Tibetan guide turned and gave a sympathetic look to Harrison, who was obviously struggling to keep up. "Mr. Harrison, are you okay? We need to walk for two more kilometers."

"Yeah, I'm okay. How often do you walk this path?"

"Every day, sir. I make my living because of tourists like you who visit the monasteries around here."

"You go alone while walking back, right? Is it boring?"

"No, sir! I sing, you know. All the R. D. Burman songs, sir." The guide blushed a little bit.

Harrison wanted to ask who that Burman was but decided on the contrary.

"R. D. Burman was a famous Bollywood music director, sir. I sing Bollywood songs all the time. Do you want to hear it?"

"It's okay. I won't understand much. Thanks for the offer though."

Bollywood was slang for the movie industry in Bombay, the city in Central India. Its influence had spread across to India's neighboring countries, including Tibet.

The guide talked fast and nonstop. He listed the names of all the monasteries in the Lhasa area as if he had just memorized the names for the school exam. Then, he passionately talked about his school days in the Sera monastery. "You will surely like Sera monastery, sir. The monks are kind; they speak English very well, sir."

Harrison wondered why there were so many *sirs*. "Did you study English there? You speak well."

The guide blushed again. His eyes were lit up with pride. "Thank you, sir. I appreciate it, sir!"

Now, they turned slightly to the right to climb a gentle slope. Harrison was awed by the breathtaking landscape on both sides of the walking path. "I see lots of roses here!"

"Yes, sir. These are wild roses, sir. That's why the monastery is called Sera Monastery. *Sera* means 'wild roses.' You know, when the monastery was built in 1419, it was surrounded by wild roses. So, they named the monastery Sera. In 1959, the Chinese government started a revolt and destroyed Sera. You know, hundreds of monks were killed inside the monastery—"

The guide abruptly stopped walking. He looked sad. He looked up at the sky and pressed his palms together as if he were praying. After a few seconds, he started walking without saying a word.

Harrison silently walked behind the guide, who was deep in thought.

"Sometimes, I wonder if there *is* a God, you know," the guide resumed his conversation.

"I don't know. I want to find out." Harrison removed his eyeglasses and wiped the dust with his shirt as he climbed and wondered how long he had to walk.

"Good luck with that, sir! I am sure monks have a lot to say on that subject."

After fifteen more minutes of brisk walking, they reached the Sera Monastery. The monastery was surrounded by many small cottages, which were, in turn, surrounded by numerous wild roses. The cottages were basically small huts made of bamboo, mud, and palm leaves.

As he walked behind the guide toward the entrance to the monastery, he heard a calming bell sound coming from one of the cottages on his right. He spotted a huge golden tower decorated with colorful cloths on the monastery's roof. A monumental tower added a divine look to the otherwise boring architecture of the monastery, which had been built using small rocks. Some of them were painted red, and some were left alone to linger with their own muddy gray.

The guide stopped in front of a giant-sized, floor-to-ceiling, twenty-foot door. He moved to the far-right corner of the door to reach a reverse-L-shaped rocky structure mounted firmly on the ground. A medium-sized copper bell hung from the top of the structure by a metal hook. The guide pulled the colorful, double-braided cotton rope, which was suspended from the center of the bell. He pulled it again as if he loved the sound coming from the copper bell. He was about to pull it again when the wooden front door was opened with a creaky sound. A man, five-foot-four, maybe thirty years old, with a clean-shaven head, fully covered in a hand-woven red robe, emerged and looked at Harrison with probing eyes.

The guide bowed and said, "This is Mr. Harrison. He is here for the meditation course."

The man bowed with his palms closed. "My name is Monk Bagya Pravava. I am the director for the residential course here. I am glad you were able to safely make it here. May I ask, how do you know about our Monastery?"

"A friend in Brazil recommended that I take the meditation course from your Monastery."

"God bless your friend!" Monk Bagya smiled warmly and politely signaled for Harrison to follow.

Although the building looked dirty from the outside, it was kept very clean inside. It was also much bigger than it looked from the outside. A good aroma—a combination of jasmine flowers and incense—filled the air. After they crossed two hundred feet from the front entrance and turned left slightly, a huge open space welcomed them. In the middle of the open space, he spotted a square-shaped stage, eight foot by eight foot by four foot, made of rock with four small steps on the front edge. Four monks sat cross-legged on the stage. One of them stood up and climbed down from the stage using the small sculpted steps when he saw them.

Monk Bagya bowed to the monk standing before him. "This is our guest, Mr. Harrison. He traveled all the way from America." He turned to Harrison and said, "This is Monk Dharma. He is the head of the monastery."

Monk Dharma bowed and said, "I pray God gives you enough strength to overcome the tragedy you have gone through."

Harrison's eyes twitched as he sensed a tickle in his chest. Monk Dharma gently touched Harrison's head with his right palm. "Trust me; you are in the right place. Monk Bagya will take care of you for the next eight weeks. I will see you at the end of the course. May God be with you." He bowed.

Harrison bowed before turning around and following Monk Bagya. As they walked toward the front door, he wondered how Monk Dharma would know about the tragedy when he had not said a word about it.

Monk Bagya turned left after coming out through the front door and briskly walked without looking back. Harrison walked slowly behind and observed the surroundings. Cold air was blowing from the mountains in the north. He asked, "It's so cold here. How can you survive this without wearing any sweaters?"

Monk Bagya turned, looked at him for a moment, and kept walking. "It's all in the mind, Mr. Harrison. You will discover it in a week. If the cold is unbearable, you can wear a triple robe."

When he had signed up for the meditation course, wearing a hand-woven robe was not part of the plan. He started wondering about the scary possibility of wearing the hand-woven robe and walking barefoot. His thoughts about his future wardrobe were interrupted when Monk

Bagya stopped before a bamboo hut and said, "This is your cottage. Please go in. I will follow you."

Harrison was disappointed even before entering the hut. It looked small. The feeling of getting ripped off grew even stronger once he was inside the cottage. There was nothing. The hut was made mostly of mud, bamboo, and palm leaves. It was empty except for a few bamboo mats on the floor, a couple of books on the shelf, and a big mud pot in the corner. Apparently, the door was the window. He placed his backpack in the corner and looked around.

"Are you looking for a pillow, Mr. Harrison?"

"Yep. You read my mind. I can give you that!"

"I believe that you would be looking for a blanket as well?"

Now, he recognized the sarcasm. He stared at the smiling monk.

"Sorry to sound rude, Mr. Harrison. We have certain rules here. There is no pillow or blanket. You need to practice sleeping on the bamboo mat. You can use your hands as a pillow for the first few days until you get used to sleeping without a pillow. If you close the door, you won't feel any cold inside. You do not need a blanket. We will teach you how to control your body temperature using your mind. Once you learn that, you will not need a sweater. Please join us for dinner in the main building in two hours. We expect more guests in this cottage by tomorrow."

More guests! No kidding.

"How many people are going to stay in this hut?"

"Three guests including you. Our program focuses on combined mental strength. We have chosen your friends in this cottage based on your profile. I am sure you will not regret our choices. Please trust me. You will feel at home very soon."

Harrison gave him a disgusted look. But the monk did not appear offended. Instead, he bowed and said, "I will see you at dinner."

Harrison did not bow. He was angry and confused. He just nodded.

He threw the backpack inside the hut and made sure his wallet and phone were in his pants pocket. Then, he walked around the cottages. There were more than twenty cottages, each spaced apart by about a hundred feet. He spotted a well-built, Caucasian man, standing on one leg with his eyes closed in front of a cottage to his left. The man appeared to be mouthing something. Harrison moved closer. The man opened his eyes after hearing the footsteps coming toward him.

He smiled warmly. "Welcome to the monastery. I am Trent Trainor. Australian. I assume you are from South America?"

"California, actually." Harrison introduced himself.

"Cool. You just arrived?"

"Yep. I was thrown in a hut. Just wondering if there is any bathroom around here."

Trent pointed at the main building of the monastery. "There are many toilets and showers in the back of the building. Just go around. You won't miss it. There are signs. You need to squat though, mind it!" He laughed loudly.

"Squatting? huh, I guess I can survive that. I tried that in Singapore airport just for the practice. I hope there is no water shortage here."

"No worries for the water. We live in the Himalayas! There is always water here. Pure water."

He thanked him and moved on. Trent Trainor resumed his one-legged pose, closed his eyes, and chanted mantras.

Chapter 18

Two hours later, Harrison sat on a pile of rocks overlooking the Himalayan Mountains spreading from north to west and watched the sun setting. Bright-orange light radiated around the mountain and gently mixed with the dark-blue sky. A loud bell sound from the Monastery reverberated and produced a sense of tranquility. Monks and guests scattered all over the place stopped what they were doing and started walking toward the monastery. Trent, the guy standing on one leg earlier, emerged from his cottage and walked toward Harrison.

"Hey, buddy, hear the bell? That's the dinner bell!" Trent grinned.

"I assume there will be a bell for breakfast and lunch as well?"

"Nope." He shook his head. "Only for dinner. We do group meditation before dinner. That's why monks try to gather everyone in the ashram." He noticed the question in Harrison's face and then added, "*Ashram* means school. For us, that building..." He pointed at the monastery. "That is the *ashram*."

When they reached the front entrance, they were greeted by a group of monks standing in line. Trent signaled Harrison to follow him to the open space area inside the monastery.

There were about fifty guests sitting on the rocky floor of the open space in one long row. Each of them faced an empty silver plate and a small silver bowl.

He heard another bell. Trent looked at him and pointed at the empty space on the floor. They sat without speaking a word. A monk came toward them quickly and placed silver plates and bowls in front of them.

The monks scattered around the monastery lined up together and sat directly opposite of guests. No one spoke a word, although all the monks smiled using their eyes. A few of them placed wooden bowls in front of them and started drumming those bowls gently with a wooden stick.

A monk, presumably a leader of the pack, said something loudly. Harrison did not understand a word of it. Then, all the monks started humming "Ohm…"

Trent Trainor shot him a quick glance before closing his eyes and humming the mantra along with the rest of the crowd.

Harrison wanted to hum along but felt weird saying something he did not understand. Every soul inside the building had closed eyes and was chanting "ohm." A gorgeous full moon was clearly visible. There was no roof above. He wondered what would happen to the group dinner party on the rainy days.

The chanting continued. He slowly closed his eyes to go with the flow. Monks seemed to be chanting a little more slowly and differently than guests. He wondered how long the chanting would go on. He felt hungry and remembered the burrito-like food he had eaten before his trekking adventure to the monastery. The burrito disappeared into a tunnel, and a divine aroma filled the air. Chanting was no longer a noise. He felt complete darkness, as if someone had switched off all the lights. The chanting gently reverberated in his head. He wished the chanting would continue forever. He did not feel hungry anymore.

A bell sounded in the distance, then, another.

He opened his eyes. Everyone had stopped chanting.

"Thank you for meditating with us," the leader of the pack said. "We all want to thank God for providing the food to us. We are all blessed to live the life we have. Every day is a blessing! Please close your eyes again for a minute and count your blessings. Think about your family, parents, spouse, children, and friends. Think about how God has enriched your lives."

Harrison closed his eyes. In the middle of the darkness, Taryn appeared, wearing a white bridal dress, in the backdrop of the church in Las Vegas. Then, she waved and smiled. Two men wearing FBI coats sat across from him and said, "We are sorry for your loss."

Count my blessings? I have none.

He tried to control the tears bubbling from his deep-blue eyes and failed. He bawled from his stomach. His sudden crying bounced off the monastery's walls and touched the hearts of everyone inside.

Chapter 19

December 1997

Stanford University came to full life as students started walking briskly toward the main quad. Taryn pushed her bike pedals quickly and maneuvered her way to avoid bumping into students walking fast to reach their classes on time. She locked her bike in a bike stand just outside McClelland Building and stared at the lock for a second. Two bikes had been stolen the previous day. Bike thefts had become quite common at all the universities, especially Stanford. The complex was open to anyone. Any John Doe could casually walk in, kneel over the wheel as if he were inspecting the tire pressure, pick the lock, and loot the bike in less than two minutes. The bike stand was not visible from the busy road. Thieves could use the quiet lane behind the main building to work their magic and disappear with the bike.

She pulled on her lock one more time to make sure it was secure. Then, she started walking toward the rear entrance of McClelland. She let the door close behind her and climbed the stairs to the third level. She turned left and walked into room 301. The door sign indicated the name of the class that was in session: Advanced Derivatives. Taryn slowed her pace, smiled at the students sitting closer to the door, and looked around. The classroom was small. Desks were arranged in conference-room style. Professor Larry stood in the center of the room with a clicker in his hand and gestured Taryn to the empty chair to the left of him.

She walked around the room, lowered herself into the plastic chair, glanced to the left, and smiled at a young man in blue jeans and green T-shirt. His eyes lit up.

Professor Larry pulled up a PowerPoint slide on the projector screen. Lots of charts were displayed on the screen. "To continue on where we left off yesterday, here is a quick look at all the advanced options. The top left shows covered call, then covered puts, then uncovered puts, also known as naked puts…" He paused for a moment to let the laughter die down. He adjusted the brim of his glasses and scanned the class. "Wall Street always tends to be sexy. Some genius named this type of derivative as naked put to catch folks' attention. Then, the name stayed on!" he said with a little smile. He continued the lecture for the next ninety minutes.

The class ended at forty-five minutes past eight o'clock. Taryn placed her right elbow on the desk and turned her gaze to the young man. "What was that about?"

"What?" Harrison looked puzzled.

"You kept on sighing during the class. Stress getting to you again?"

He shook his head. "It's not stress. It's the professor's accent," he said in a low voice. "The class is hard enough to understand with all these *calls* and *puts*. His accent makes it even more difficult."

Taryn giggled as she grabbed the laptop and shoved it into her backpack. "Understood. Don't stress out too much, Harry! Care to grab a coffee?"

"Sure."

As they walked toward the door, Professor Larry looked at her and raised his hand. "Taryn, can I talk to you for a minute?"

"Yeah, sure." She signaled for Harrison to wait and walked closer to the center of the room.

"I have a TA position opening up. I need someone to take care of financial accounting. The course starts in the spring. Are you interested?"

"Yeah, sure, of course!" She wanted to scream with joy.

"Good. I'll email you the details."

"Thanks!"

She observed the spark in Harrison's eyes as they moved down the stairs and raised a brow.

"TA? That's super cool! Is that course for undergraduates?"

"Yeah, I put in my request last quarter. I'm glad it came through. It's going to help me with the bills."

"Yeah!" he said as he opened the door leading to Carlos Street. "I'm super happy for you!"

"I can see that in your pretty blue eyes!" Taryn smiled and walked out.

A group of graduate students walked to the business

center across the street. She crossed her arms and looked up at the sun, which was partially covered by the clouds. "The world is so beautiful, isn't it?"

"The world is even more beautiful with ice cream! Let's go celebrate your TA award!" He smiled.

She was mesmerized by his smile. His teeth protruded a little when he smiled, which added more charm. She looked into his eyes and hugged him. "You're a good friend, Harry!"

"I'm bribing you with ice cream so that you will help me with those fancy derivatives."

She giggled. "*You silly*. Let's go."

As they walked toward Green Library Cafeteria, she asked, "What are you doing for summer? Going to Brazil again?"

"No. I asked my parents to visit me here. I am seriously trying to get into Goldman Sachs. Can you believe these guys are so selective even for interns?"

Taryn nodded as they turned right onto Galvez Street. "All these people are like that. Well, the Stanford name gives us a strong edge though. My sister works in McKinsey. She promised me that she would get me in there." She shook her head and laughed. "She never keeps her promises. So, I don't have too much hope!"

Chapter 20
April 2000

It feels like I proposed to you just yesterday!" Harrison said as Taryn kept trying to pacify their little daughter.

"Hmm...did you say something?"

He laughed. "Oh, God! Now that April is born, you've totally forgotten me. Whatever I say, I have to repeat many times before it sinks in for you!"

She was not sure if he was sarcastic or angry or both. "Hello! I have to keep reminding you. *You* are the one who could not wait for a child!" She gently patted his head.

He hugged Taryn and kissed April's forehead. "Yeah, I wanted the child. But this little girl stole you from me!"

"Well, she needs Mommy for the next few years."

"Really? My sister told me that girls need moms *forever*. Hmm, maybe except during the teen years."

"She's just six months old! You're talking about the teenage years already!"

"You know, with the speed our life goes…I wouldn't be surprised if April turned thirteen tomorrow!" He was silent for a second before asking, "What happened with the McKinsey interview? Did those people call you?"

Taryn shook her head. "Yes and no. They are interested, but they'll need some time. My sister promised me that it would be Okay. I *still* don't trust her!" Her wide grin showed bright white teeth.

"Your sister may surprise you. You never know!" After a moment of thought, he said, "Are you sure McKinsey is the right choice? You would need to travel a lot. Are you okay with that? You should find something that does not involve travel, at least until April goes to school."

She leaned on him and kissed him. "You know, I am kind of obsessed with McKinsey. I don't know why. But it feels like that is my destiny."

"It's not *destiny*. It's just your obsession! You want to show you're as good as your sister."

"Whatever you want to call it! But if I get McKinsey, I will take it!"

He half-smiled and nodded.

~

April played with Barney and friends in the living room. Taryn kept an eye on her as she poured the coffee into a small porcelain cup placed on the kitchen island. She looked at Harrison and hesitated for a moment. "I am going for a conference in New York on Sunday. I'll be back on Tuesday."

"Oh, not again!" He sighed. "It's been a year since you joined McKinsey. You've taken more than ten trips already. Why are these guys asking you to travel every month?"

"Well, because I am the smartest! You know what? I'm actually excited about this. I haven't been to New York for almost twenty years."

"Well, yeah, I guess."

"What are you worried about?"

"Well, I am going to miss you for three days. April is going to miss you a lot."

"I'm going to miss April more than she would ever miss me! I think we should have delayed kids, you know, until we were settled into our careers. What do you think?"

"Isn't it too late for that discussion?" He hugged her from behind and kissed her.

"No time for romance, Harry! Go and get ready for your wonderful commute!"

～

San Francisco's airport buzzed with hundreds of passengers in Terminal 2. A tall brunette in Gate 22 announced, "We're boarding for flight number 71 to New York in a minute. We request first-class passengers and families with infants to come forward."

Harrison hoped Taryn would change her mind and cancel the trip. "Do you really need to go?"

She didn't reply directly. Instead, she hugged and kissed him before handing April over to him.

April started crying and leaped back to Taryn.

"Oh, baby! Don't cry. Listen, I'll be back in a minute, you know. I need to go in and check if everyone is inside the flight and run back to you, okay?"

Harrison laughed. "That is so lame!"

She squeezed his hands. "April is so sweet. Dad will take good care of you. I will be back soon."

She stopped before entering the gate, turned around, and winked at Harrison. "Be a good boy, Harry! Bye, April!"

He just realized that he had not seen her winking for a long time. The twinkle in her eyes mesmerized him.

~

He got a call from Taryn on the following Tuesday. "Sorry to wake you up early. I'm at JFK. Flight leaves in thirty minutes. I can't wait to see you!"

"Tell me about it! April is asking me when you're coming back every five minutes."

She laughed. "Really? I'll be there soon. Bye, honey!"

"Bye!" He hung up and looked at the clock, which flashed 5:45 a.m. He had been awake until midnight taking care of April, who had a high fever and kept asking for her mother. He stretched his legs on the couch, closed his eyes, and drifted to sleep. It was nine o'clock when he woke up. He walked to April's bedroom and slowly opened the door. She was still sleeping. Her temperature had come down a little to 101° Fahrenheit.

He walked to the kitchen and poured coffee into a tall mug. The coffee would compensate for the lack of sleep. He thought about calling the nanny to ask her to come in sooner but instead decided to call his manager. He pulled the mobile phone from his pajamas and dialed. "Hey, Greg, I need to take the day off. My daughter is not well. Sorry for the short notice."

"Actually, I am advising everyone to work from home

today. Did you see the news? There was a terrorist attack in New York." Greg's voice was shaking.

"What? In New York? My wife is there."

"Don't worry. Taryn will be okay. Where does she stay?"

"She should be in the air by now."

There was silence on the other side, uncomfortable silence. Greg finally broke it and asked, "Which airline did she take?"

"United."

Again, there was silence. "Greg, is there anything wrong?" He hated the silence.

"Hmm, nothing, do you know the flight number, Harrison?"

"Flight number 93. What happened? Why are you acting weird?" He was agitated.

There was silence again.

He abruptly hung up without waiting for Greg's response and then called Taryn.

Her phone kept ringing. No answer.

Terrorist attack. His heart raced fast like never before.

His head hurt as he sat on the corner of the couch and fired up the television remote on the side table. The television screen showed September 11 in the top right. Breaking news kept scrolling at the bottom of the screen.

> United Flight 175 and American Airlines Flight 11 crashed into the World Trade Center. United Flight 93 crashed into a field in Somerset County, Pennsylvania, killing all passengers and crew aboard.

Chapter 21

September 2004

April waved. "Bye, Daddy!" before going into her classroom. Harrison smiled, waved back, and slowly walked to the car.

"Is she your only child?"

Harrison turned around to see a lean, tall woman.

"Hi, I'm Ms. Williams, the principal." She shook his hand warmly. "Don't worry. We will take good care of your little angel!"

"Oh, I'm sure you will! Sorry, was that too obvious?" Harrison wondered.

"You mean, seeing you concerned?"

"Yeah. Am I the only father worried about leaving a child in the school?"

"You would be surprised. Kids take it cool. Parents take it harder though!"

"Maybe. My wife used to tell me guys become soft once they have daughters."

"Yeah, I heard that too. Is it true?"

"In my case, it's true. I was already soft. After April was born, I became softer. Almost to the point of being scared of everything when it comes to her."

"I'm sure your wife will balance you out. I bet she isn't as anxious as you!" Ms. Williams chuckled.

Harrison paused for a moment and sighed. "Actually, she is gone. She was killed on 9/11."

Ms. Williams was visibly shaken. Her smile immediately disappeared. She gasped for a second. Then, she touched Harrison's shoulder. "Oh…I am so sorry. I can't even imagine what you are going through."

Harrison saw tears were starting to come out of Ms. Williams's eyes. She had looked so strong just a minute ago.

"Thanks, Ms. Williams. This is a difficult time for us. I really hope that school will let April forget what she lost."

"Yes, sure, Mr. Harrison. Please take care." Ms. Williams shook his hand and walked toward the school office.

Harrison looked in the direction of the classroom and sighed. He walked slowly to the car, lowered himself into the driver's seat, and smiled wryly at the elderly woman who sat in the passenger seat.

"You look sad, Harry."

"No, Mom. I am not sad. I'm just thinking about what April is doing." Harrison started the car.

His mother smiled. "I'm sure April has made a friend already. She is such a happy child!"

Harrison nodded and added, "Thanks, Mom, for coming over. I wouldn't have survived without you after Taryn was gone."

She controlled her tears and looked at the passing trees on the right. She looked at the blue sky and said, "Taryn was a wonderful person. I miss her a lot."

Harrison slowed the car and stopped at a traffic light. "I don't know if all this is cruelty or fate. God gave me a wonderful life but took it back just like that…"

She looked at him. "Life is very unpredictable, Son. There must be a reason for everything."

The traffic light turned green.

"I don't believe that. What could be the reason for taking Taryn away from me? Hmm? Forget me; taking her away from *April* is very cruel. I don't believe in God anymore, Mom." He pushed the accelerator pedal and sped up the car.

His mother didn't say anything. It was difficult to believe in anything when loved ones were suddenly taken away.

Harrison looked at his mother sniffling. "What happened?"

"Hmm, nothing. I was just thinking maybe…if you had stayed in Rio, your life would have been better. You don't need to go through this."

"That's not true, Mom. I don't think I would have been happy if I hadn't met Taryn. We were married for only two years, but I feel like I knew her forever! I don't think anyone else could have given me the happiness she gave me."

Tears flowed down from her eyes.

"Why are you crying now, Mom?"

His mom sniffled. "I don't know how you are going to bring up April all alone. Poor girl lost her mother already."

"I am not alone, Mom! You're here, remember?" Harrison tried to cheer her up.

"Hmm, but for how long? I have a visa only for six months. I will be gone in three months."

"We will see. My lawyer told me we can ask for an extension." He turned around in the corner. "Okay, Mom. You have the keys, right? I'll be back by six o'clock. I'll pick up April on the way. Vegetables are in the fridge. Call me if you need anything."

His mother got out of the car slowly. "Okay. Bye, Harry."

Twenty-two minutes later, Harrison pulled his Honda Accord into the parking lot of Palo Alto Business Center. His Blackberry chirped. There was a text message from Russell Edison, chief financial officer of his start-up. "We're ready and waiting for you." Harrison quickly pulled his laptop bag from the front seat, clicked the car remote to lock the car, and briskly walked toward the main building. A minute later, he pushed the elevator button and waited. He was ten minutes late already, and there was no sign of the elevator coming down. He lost his patience, walked to his left, and climbed the stairs fast to reach his office on the fourth floor.

As he swung open the door, the receptionist smiled. He nodded gently and walked toward the conference room facing east. The conference room had a big oval table, which was surrounded by numerous leather chairs. Everyone looked his way as he entered the room. Investment bankers from Goldman Sachs sat on one side of the table. The other side was occupied by his management team.

He apologized as he walked toward the only vacant chair in the center of the table. "Sorry, folks. The 101 is totally backed up. I think this is another sign the economy is picking up in the Bay Area!"

Everyone laughed.

"Did you check the housing prices on the peninsula? Even a two-bedroom condominium in San Mateo goes for four hundred and fifty thousand!" an Asian woman sitting in the corner said.

Everyone laughed again.

"No kidding!"

Harrison felt happier when he saw everyone in a good mood. He had quit his job in Cisco after Taryn died to take care of April. He did not want to leave her in day care. He had worked from home as a consultant for a few months before he came up with an algorithm to shrink the amount of disk space needed for computer data. He had founded a storage networking company from his garage three years ago. He got his first client in five months when he proved that his start-up could reduce the storage needs by a factor of twenty. Six months later, he got funding from a top-notch venture capital company in Palo Alto. He was able to distract his mind from the personal tragedy; work became his therapy. The start-up grew ninety percent every year and got serious attention from Wall Street in less than two years.

Rocky Davidson, a well-built guy in his thirties, stood up and shook Harrison's hand. "Thanks, Harry, for giving us the opportunity to take your company public." Rocky was a Stanford Graduate School of Business (GSB) alumnus. He had met Harrison back in the fall of 1995, when he interviewed him as part of the Stanford GSB admission process. The two had remained good friends since then.

Rocky clicked his mouse to start the PowerPoint presentation. "We'll start the road show next Monday. Here is our game plan!" For the next ninety minutes, he detailed the plan to cover twelve cities before taking the company public in the NASDAQ stock exchange in December.

"Our plan is to decide final pricing by early December. The first trading session will likely be in the second week of December. The stock will start trading just in time for the Santa Claus rally! If all goes well, we will see a sexy price jump on the first trading day!" As Rocky concluded his presentation, everyone applauded.

Harrison put the phone alarm to snooze and tried to go back to sleep. He had been awake until one o'clock in the morning preparing for the upcoming road show. April had to be at the school by eight o'clock sharp. It had been only two months since she started school. She loved everything about it, except getting the late pass from the school office. "April is very punctual even at this age!" his mother had said proudly at dinner the previous night.

He felt the soft pillow on his leg as he stared at the ceiling. April hit him with the pillow. "Hey, Dad! Get up! Remember, I go to school!"

Harrison pushed his head to the bed's headrest and stretched his legs. "Come here, my angel." He extended his arms toward her.

April ran to him, jumped on his lap, and squeezed his nose. "Why are you still sleeping? You are not responsible, you know."

Harrison laughed. "Really? Who is responsible then? Would that be you?"

April shook her head. "*No, silly*. Mommy!" She pointed her little finger to Taryn's portrait on the wall behind the bed frame. Then, she put her head down and was silent in sadness.

Harrison quickly broke the silence. "Well, Mommy taught me to be responsible. I will try to be more responsible, okay?"

"Okay. Now get ready and drop me at the school!" She grabbed his eyeglasses from the side table and used both her hands to place them on the bridge of his nose.

He adjusted the rim of the glasses, picked up April, and carried her to the living room. "Mom, I'll be ready in fifteen minutes. April needs lunch. I have a lot of meetings today. I arranged for the school bus from today. Only for the return trip. You remember the bus stop, Mom?"

His mother smiled. "Yes. You have shown me twenty times already. I know how to walk from there to here."

It was six minutes before eight o'clock when Harrison reached the school. He could see Ms. Williams in the distance. She was giving instructions to all volunteer students about how to regulate traffic in the school parking lot. April got down from her seat and grabbed her backpack. "Bye, Daddy!"

Harrison waved back. April smiled and walked toward the school. He put the car in drive and slowly moved the car. Just then, he noticed April had stopped walking and was staring at him. When she saw him looking at her, she smiled again and sent a flying kiss. He waved again and watched April disappearing into the crowd.

∾

It was a new experience for Grace Azevedo. She went to the bus stop thirty minutes early and waited for the school bus. The bus came five minutes late. For the last five minutes, she had been wondering whether she was at the right bus stop. She felt relieved when she saw April climbing down from the bus. April ran to Grace and hugged her. "Hey, Grandma! How was your day? Are you bored? Do you want to see my painting? Ms. Lewis told me it's fantastic!"

Grace laughed. "Sure, let's walk to the house and eat some food. Then, I will see your painting."

"Okay. I'm sure you will love my painting."

"Of course. I know you are an artist, April!"

"Did you walk too much, Grandma?" April tilted her head sideways and smiled.

"No. It was not bad. We are almost there, dear." Grace adored April's smile.

When they reached the house, Carol, the girl living in the next house, waved her hands and ran toward April. Carol's family had moved from New York to San Jose last year. They were born in the same month a few days apart. "Hey, April, do you want to play?"

"Okay. But I need to eat first. I am *very* hungry! You know, Ms. Santos did not let us even drink water in the class."

"Really? That is mean." Carol walked with April into her house.

April threw her Minnie Mouse–themed backpack on the couch and ran to the bathroom. As she washed her hands with soap, a smile formed on her face when she remembered

Ms. Lewis dancing and singing, "Stop germs! Stay healthy! Wash your hands" in the last period. Then, she ran to the kitchen, grabbed chocolate chip cookies, and munched.

"You need to eat slow, April. At this rate, you are going to choke!" Grace came closer and adjusted the hair falling onto April's forehead.

April stopped for a second and looked up. "No, Grandma, I am just fine. You have no idea how hungry I am!" She wiped the cookie crumbs from her lips.

Grace gently ran her hands through April's hair. "I think I should wash your hair tomorrow."

"Okay, let's talk about that tomorrow. I need to go! Carol is waiting for me!" She ran to the living room and stood in front of Carol, who was obviously bored, flipping through a *Parenting* magazine that had been lying on the coffee table. "Come on; let's go!" April grabbed Carol's hand.

Grace walked across the living room and stood near the window adjacent to the front door. She watched April chasing butterflies with Carol in the small flower garden near the front porch.

She felt pain poking from inside her stomach. Since the day she came to San Jose, she had experienced the stomach pain every few days. She had hoped that pain would go away someday. But it did not. She ran to the bathroom.

Seven minutes later, she heard a loud screeching sound as she closed the bathroom door behind her.

What was that? She looked through the front window. Carol was running toward the house. Grace quickly opened the front door.

"Someone took April in the car! Someone took her!"

Carol screamed. "Call the police! Call the police!"

Grace quickly ran down to the front lawn and scanned the road. There was no sign of April and no sign of a car, except for disgusting exhaust. She shouted at Carol, who was standing behind her. "What are you saying? Who took April? She was playing with you, right?"

Carol quickly nodded. "Yes. But someone came in a car. He asked for help to find his cat. Then, he dragged April to the car and drove that way." She pointed to the far end of the street.

Grace felt dizzy. She ran into the house, grabbed the telephone handset, and frantically dialed Harrison's number.

Chapter 22

Police Detective Frank Littleton looked up. "Do you have any other recent pictures of your daughter?"

"This is a recent picture. It was taken just six months ago for April's school application." Harrison's voice was broken.

Detective Littleton turned his attention toward the middle-aged woman holding Carol's hands. He asked, "Ma'am, do you mind if we ask your daughter a few questions?"

She nodded.

He pulled a bar stool up and sat closer to Carol, who sat on the couch.

"Carol, can you tell us again what happened?"

Carol looked at Harrison and turned to the detective. "We were just playing. Then, a blue car came on the road. A man got down and asked us, 'Did you see my cat?'"

"Okay. The guy lost his cat? He asked you about his cat?" The detective took his notes.

Carol nodded. "Yes. We didn't see any cat. We told him that. Then…"

"Then?"

"He asked us if we could help him to find the cat. April said she could help. Then…" Carol stopped for a second and sniffled. "He asked April to come with him to look for the cat. April was walking to the car. Then, he grabbed her, opened the back door, put her in the backseat, and drove…I ran to April's grandma and told her what happened."

The detective looked at Carol. "You are very helpful, Carol. Thank you. Did April say anything? Did April know this guy? Have you seen this guy before?"

Carol shook her head. "I don't know. April was crying. She put her head on the car window and cried. She kept saying, '*Tell my dad.*'"

Tears fell down Harrison's face and ripped his heart.

"Do you remember the car color, Carol?"

"Yeah, it was blue. Just like this blue." Carol pointed at the couch.

"Okay. Navy blue. Was it a small car or big car?"

"It's small. Just like our car."

"Okay. Small car. If you see this guy again, will you be able to identify him?" The detective posed his question gently.

"Identify?"

"I mean, if you see him again, can you show him to us?"

"Yes, I will. I remember his face." Carol looked confident.

"Did you notice any other details? Any scars on his face?

Anything else you can tell us about this guy? Or the car?"

Carol looked up at the ceiling and thought about something for a moment. Then, she spoke in a tremulous voice. "He was kind of short. He wore glasses. He walked weird. His right leg was a little crooked."

"Like he was crippled?" the detective asked.

Carol nodded. Her mother gently pressed her hands.

"Anything else you can remember, Carol?"

"I don't know. There was a big Hot Wheels sticker on the car door. That's all I saw." Carol put her head down, stared at her pink-colored fingernails, and pressed her right thumb on her index fingernail. April had painted her nails pink last week. The nail polish still remained fresh.

"Thanks, Carol." The detective signaled his deputy and said, "Get the sketch artist. Carol may help us find this guy. I want the artist to draw the sketch ASAP. Once we get it, we need to distribute that to the media. This guy is probably local to the area."

The detective turned to Harrison. "Mr. Azevedo, do you have any custodial issues?"

Harrison wiped his tears and shook his head. "No. My wife died on 9/11."

"Oh, sorry. Do you have any enemies or—"

"No." Harrison sobbed. He could not believe April had been taken away from him. He had called 911 as soon as his mother had called him. His heart was pounding like hell when he drove home. The cops were already in the house when he reached it.

The detective broke the silence. "We issued the Amber

Alert already. We will send the picture to the media. We hope to find your daughter soon. FBI folks are on their way. They are always involved whenever there is a child abduction."

Harrison pressed his right palm to his forehead. "I never thought this could happen to me. *Please* catch this bastard and get my daughter back...*Please.*"

The detective touched Harrison's shoulder with compassion. "I hope that we catch this guy soon. Carol has seen this guy. Once we get the sketch of this guy, we should be moving very quickly." He reassured him again. "We will catch this guy."

Harrison felt intense pain in his heart as if an elephant had sat on his chest. He struggled to breathe. His entire world looked blank.

Chapter 23

Biana Patterson placed a leather folder on the dining room table and smiled at the old couple sitting in the bright-orange seat. "Here is your check. You can pay it at the front counter. Drive safe; it's Friday night!"

The couple smiled and waved back without saying a word.

The big analog clock on the wall of the Denny's restaurant indicated ten minutes past eleven o'clock. As she walked back toward the kitchen, she stopped when she saw the picture on the television. It was a sketch of a man with eyeglasses. The face looked familiar.

She ignored patrons walking on her side and focused on the news anchors. "Five-year-old April Azevedo was kidnapped at four o'clock today in San Jose. The suspect is a Hispanic male in his forties. He wears thick eyeglasses. He may be crippled or have suffered an injury to his right leg. If you know about the person shown in the sketch, please call 911 or the FBI hotline." The phone numbers flashed on the screen.

Biana gasped and shook her head in disgust. She walked quickly toward the front counter. Allison, her coworker, was taking a phone order from a customer. Biana pulled the headset from Allison's ear and disconnected the call. "Sorry, Allison. This is an emergency." She ignored Allison's frightened, pale face and dialed 911.

"Hello, this is about the girl kidnapped today. I know the guy shown on the television just now. He is my ex-boyfriend." She went on to provide more details. "Yes, I am at Denny's, just off Holly Road Exit on 101. My shift ends in six hours."

Allison put her right hand on her forehead and listened as Biana wrapped up the call. "Okay. I'll wait right here. No worries."

As Biana hung up the phone, she observed the question in Allison's eyes. "Sorry, Allison. A girl was kidnapped this evening in San Jose. I saw the sketch of the kidnapper on the TV. It looks like my ex-boyfriend. I should have killed that bastard a long time ago." Biana tightly gripped the edge of the front desk. "I should have *killed* him."

Ten minutes later, San Mateo Police Detective Rick Kim sat across the table from Biana and wrote down the details.

"Thanks, Biana. We'll move very quickly. I hope that the address you gave us is still current."

"It must be. Juan does not have a stable job. He lives with his mother. You will find him there." Biana sounded confident.

Detective Rick Kim called the control room and broadcasted the address. He hung up and sighed. "FBI agents and Los Gatos Police will take it up from here. Thanks for your help. I'm sure you saved this little girl's life!"

Biana gave a wry smile and stared at her right palm.

The detective noticed the stress in Biana's face. "What's wrong? Is there something else we should know?"

Biana shook her head back and forth. After a few seconds of thinking, she took a deep breath before speaking. "Juan is impotent. He blamed me for his impotence. A few years ago, he tried to rape my sister, who was visiting us from Texas. We beat him up and kicked him out of the house. He never came back. Later, we found that he had tried to abuse an eleven-year-old girl in our neighborhood. The girl's family didn't file a complaint because they didn't want to deal with the all the questions from cops. The family didn't have the papers—" She paused for a moment. "You know, they crossed the border when the girl was two. They were afraid that they would run into immigration issues."

The detective sighed. "Thanks for the additional information. I'm sure it's going to be very helpful."

෨

Los Gatos Police Officer Kennedy Ross reached Juan Martinez's house at five minutes past midnight. He scanned the street as he got out of his Ford Crown Victoria. The street was very quiet and was packed with houses on both sides. He looked at the small house on his right and scanned the exterior of the house. A blue Toyota Corolla was parked in the driveway. A large-sized Hot Wheels sticker was stuck on the driver's-side door.

Four minutes later, a SWAT team from San Jose arrived. Officer Ross briefed Captain Fletcher, a well-built man in his early thirties, who led the SWAT team. Captain Fletcher signaled the two officers to wait near the back of the house and two in the front.

Ross knocked on the front door. There was no answer. He knocked again. "Open the door, Police." Ross repeated the process two times. Fletcher got ready to storm in but stopped when the light bulb lit up on the wall near the front door.

An elderly woman opened the door. "Police? What happened?" She rubbed her terrified eyes.

Ross spoke. "Ma'am, we want to talk to Juan Martinez. Where is he?"

"Juan is my son. He is sleeping." Garcia Martinez's hands trembled. "What is going on?"

Ross did not answer. Instead, he quickly moved into the house and scanned. The kitchen was in the far end. There was one room on the right and one on the left. He stormed into the room on the right and found the man in a deep sleep.

Fletcher switched on the light. Ross checked for any weapon within the reach of the man and knocked on the bed frame. "Juan!" His loud voice rattled the man.

Juan jerked and sat up on the bed. His eyes widened when he saw Fletcher's gun pointed straight at his face.

"Are you Juan Martinez?" Ross asked.

"Yes." Juan scanned the room and noticed more officers coming into the room. "Why are you here? What is going on?"

An officer whispered to Fletcher, "We searched the entire house. There is no sign of the girl."

Fletcher walked closer to Juan. "Where is April?" He was ready to kick him.

"April? I don't know what you are talking about." Juan shook his head.

"Where were you this evening? Around four o'clock?" Ross asked.

"I don't remember. I was just roaming around, looking for work. I guess I was in Home Depot." Juan shook his head again. His body was shaking.

"Were you shopping in Home Depot?"

"No. I am a handyman. I look for work outside Home Depot. I think you are mistaken. I did not take any girl. I am not that kind of a person." He looked up at the ceiling and avoided eye contact with Ross.

"We did not say anything about *taking* a girl. Let me ask you again. Where is April?" Ross was ready to punch him in the face.

Juan shook his head. "I don't know."

Ross removed handcuffs from his duty belt, pulled Juan's hands behind his back, and clipped the cuff. Then, he read him his Miranda rights. "You have the right to remain silent when questioned. Anything you say or do may be used against you in a court of law. You have the right to consult an attorney before speaking to the police and to have an attorney present during questioning now or in the future."

Fletcher gazed at Juan. *Sick bastard, I wish I had a right to put a bullet in your head.*

Chapter 24

An hour later, Assistant Special Agent Joshua Theaker sat across the table from Juan Martinez in Los Gatos Police Department's holding room. "Juan, there is no point in lying about it. We found the girl's bracelet in your car. We have an eyewitness. If we find the girl alive, you will spend less time in prison. Think about it."

Juan was silent.

Theaker hated the silence. He clenched his fists and struggled to control himself. "Where is April?"

Juan looked up and smiled. "I don't know." He shrugged. "Where is my lawyer?"

Theaker ground his teeth. *Bastard is lawyering up. Free lawyers for criminals. What a waste of taxpayers' money.*

"I believe that your lawyer will arrive for your funeral." Theaker surprised himself by saying that.

The smirk disappeared from Juan's face. His eyes widened in horror. Theaker liked it. "You know, Juan, only in America you have the freedom to kidnap an innocent girl and ask for a *free lawyer*. I hope that you rot in *hell* along with your lawyer."

Juan folded his lips and looked down.

Theaker walked out of the holding room and went straight to a small conference room on the right. As he opened the glass door, Assistant Special Agent Kimberly Walck and Officer Kennedy Ross looked up. The Los Gatos map was laid on the conference room table.

"Anything?" Kimberly Walck raised her eyebrow.

Theaker shook his head and sighed. "That sicko is not saying a word. He just lawyered up!" He stood right across the table from Officer Ross and said, "It has been nine hours since the girl was kidnapped. The more time we lose, there is much less chance of finding the girl alive."

Walck turned to Ross. "We need to find out if this guy has another house or a place where he could hide the girl."

Ross shook his head. "I don't think so. Juan is a temporary worker. His mother does not work. They're renting the house. These folks live paycheck to paycheck. I don't think this guy has another place to hide the girl."

Theaker nodded and said, "*Unless*...there is a free place for this bastard to hide the girl." He noticed the sadness in Kimberly Walck's face and knew the reason.

More often than not, the FBI team found the victims in the remote parts of state parks or in the mountains. Most of the time, the victims were found dead.

Theaker looked down and ran his right index finger across the surface of the map. "April was kidnapped from here." He ran his finger down and stopped at a point where

"Los Gatos" was written in big red letters. "Juan's house is here. He took the girl at four o'clock. He was arrested at midnight. So, he had about six to seven hours to hide the girl. We need to search the lakes, state parks, and mountains around all these areas." He circled the areas surrounding San Jose and Los Gatos. "We should start with these areas and expand to Santa Cruz if needed."

The San Francisco FBI team divided themselves into three groups, each focusing on different cities: Los Gatos, San Jose, and Campbell. Theaker asked for assistance from the Sacramento and Los Angeles FBI teams; they were on their way. He instructed local police departments to request volunteers for the search.

Five minutes past six o'clock in the morning, the search was started in Lexington Hills, Vasona Lake, and El Sereno Open Space Reserve simultaneously. As more volunteers joined the effort, the search expanded to Scotts Valley in the south and Woodside in the east.

Theaker received the call at eleven o'clock. Hikers had found the dead body of a young girl on Guadalupe Trail, hidden behind the bushes.

Theaker and Walck reached the trail at noon. Walck's heart stopped for a second when she saw the girl's lifeless body lying on the muddy ground, facing the cloudy sky. April looked like an angel just fallen from the sky.

Chapter 25

Present Day

April threw her hands out the window. "Tell my dad! Tell my dad..." The blue Toyota Corolla sped past. The driver kept his left hand on the steering wheel, turned his head to the backseat, and used his right hand to pull April down onto the backseat. She fell down and landed on the floor mat.

"I want my dad" she sobbed.

"*April!*" Harrison woke up with a scream. The pain in his head was intense. He pulled the bed sheet up and wiped his face. Tears poured from his eyes. He gave up on controlling the tears. Many years ago, he thought that his tears might dry out after too much crying. It did not happen. He switched on the light and checked the time. It was ten minutes past midnight.

April was found dead a day after she was kidnapped. Juan Martinez's DNA was ensconced in April's tiny fingernails. When Harrison saw Juan during the trial, the pervert smiled at him. *No regrets.*

The San Jose County district attorney sought the death penalty for the heinous crime. After many months of trial, the jury concluded that Juan was guilty. He was given a lethal injection in 2014, a full ten years after being sentenced to death. In all those years he had been allowed to live on after his victim, he had never shown any remorse for the innocent life he destroyed.

The pain spread across his shoulders and crawled all the way down his spine.

He placed the pillow upright, leaned on it, and closed eyes. He could hear his breathing. He wanted to see only blackness, but he saw Taryn. Nothing else.

He watched Taryn sitting in the window seat and staring at her laptop screen. She heard the loud thud and watched in horror as the flight attendant fell on her shoulder. She heard a scream coming from the front seats. Fire streamed past and right through her.

He felt like he was going to throw up. He slowly walked over to the bathroom and splashed cold water on his face.

He breathed hard as he sat on the bed. He switched on the television to distract his mind from replaying the tragedy.

"The FBI team found the backpack and shoes of the seven-year-old girl kidnapped in Danville. The search continues in the Mount Diablo Foothills Regional Park." Breaking news flashed on the screen.

He grabbed the alarm clock from the nightstand and threw it at the television. "Bastards…"

Why don't you target someone your own age?

Blood boiled all over his body. He looked through the

window. It was dark outside. The alarm clock lying on the floor flashed 1:00 a.m. for a second before going dark.

He took a deep breath. Then, he sat cross-legged on the bed, closed his eyes, and started to meditate. He remembered Monk Dharma and his words.

Leave it to God. Anger is evil; it will eat you alive.

Meditation helped him sleep better—but not today. He wanted to see only darkness when he closed his eyes. Instead, he saw April giggling and calling him *silly*. Taryn held his hands and walked toward Memorial Church in Stanford. A cop asked for April's picture.

He opened his eyes, stretched his legs, rolled to his left into the fetal position, and pulled the comforter up to fully cover himself. He closed his eyes. April and Carol chased butterflies.

Leave it to God? That did not work.

He sobbed and sobbed until sleep took away his misery temporarily.

Chapter 26

George Williams leaned closer to the mirror and looked at the bleeding wound below his right eye. He smiled a little as he pushed his tongue up to hit his upper mouth, which made a click sound. The blood trickled down to his neck. He looked around, removed toilet paper from the roller, soaked it under the running water, and pressed hard against the wound. *Man, it feels good.*

He stared at the blue wall as he sat on the granite counter top. *Time to party.* He made a little jump onto the vinyl floor, opened the drawer below the sink, grabbed neomycin ointment, squeezed it to get a pea-size amount, and applied it on the wound. *Fighting is good. Blood is nice.*

Then, he switched off the bathroom lights as he reentered the bedroom. A girl, in her late twenties, lay on the bed with her eyes closed. Her face looked at the ceiling; her arms and legs were spread horizontally. She showed no movement. He removed the bed sheet that covered her naked body and jumped on her.

A few minutes later, he made a little dance movement

as he slowly walked toward the kitchen and looked for something better than beer. He pulled open the door below the sink and found Drano. He opened it and pushed his face down slowly to inhale the aroma of the sink drainer. Immediately, he pushed back. The stench was different but strong. He inhaled, exhaled, and pushed his face down again. It felt better this time. He waited for a minute to let the flavor settle in his lungs. He pushed his face down again and slowly inhaled. He pulled back when his head started hurting.

The earth under him shook a little, as if there had been an earthquake. The beer bottle on the dining room table looked blurry. He grabbed it, filled it with water, and walked back into the bedroom. The girl was still unconscious. He walked closer to her, titled her head upward, and emptied the bottle on her nose.

The girl violently woke up and choked.

He moved back a little and laughed hard. The girl kept choking. He sat on the edge of the bed and stared at her until the choking came to a full stop.

Now, the girl coughed heavily and looked at him. "George, please—please let me go home. I won't tell anyone."

"Oh, dear Beth!" He rubbed his reddish eyes. "Well, you can't tell anyone because you are not leaving my house."

The girl whimpered. She tried to get up and failed. "What did you do to me? I trusted you, George. Please let me go." She put her palms together and pleaded.

He laughed again and winked. "You look good without any clothes, Beth!" He pulled the bed sheet down.

The girl fought to keep the bed sheet on. "You are a monster, bastard."

"You have no idea!" He jumped on her and landed on the bed with his left palm on the pillow, right next to her right ear. His right hand reached into his back pocket. He pulled out a sharp steel knife and slid it across her neck from right to left.

She screamed for two seconds and died. He pulled her face up and made her lips touch the wound below his eye. "Lick it. See what you did. Lick it, bitch!" He did that ritual two times before throwing her head back to the pillow.

The girl's eyes stared at the ceiling. He smiled at her dead eyes and the blood-covered pillow.

Then, he rolled over on her left, cuddled her, and slept.

∿

The alarm sounded like an ambulance siren and abruptly ended his sleep. He hit the snooze, cursed the phone, and then turned to see the girl in the pool of blood.

Shit. What a mess.

He jumped out of the bed, stared at the girl, and tried to remember what had happened. Then, he shrugged, lifted her naked body, and carried her over to the bathtub, which had been customized to add more depth.

After carefully placing her inside the tub, he walked to the walk-in closet in the corner of the bedroom. The closet was big enough to accommodate a queen-size bed, although it was used to store chemicals. It had three shelves on each side. He reached to the top shelf and donned a chemical gas mask. Then, he grabbed a bottle from the lower shelf. He walked into the bathroom, switched on the exhaust fan, and then slowly poured the sulfuric acid from the bottle into the tub.

He quickly walked out of the bathroom after emptying the bottle. He heard the bubbling sound from the tub as he closed the door. He removed the gas mask, threw it on the floor, opened the balcony door, and inhaled the fresh air. The wind blowing from San Pablo Bay chilled his face. He took a quick peek at the clock mounted on the living room wall. Ten o'clock in the morning.

He pulled out a cigarette pack and smoked it away one by one. He had about thirty minutes to kill, until the acid did its job and melted the dead girl's skin away to keep just the bones in the tub.

∼

It was the next morning. George held a Peet's coffee cup in his right hand, sipped a little, and waited for the walk signal near San Francisco State University. The Muni train was approaching the station across the street. He jumped into the street as soon as the walk signal lit up and ran toward Muni while making sure not to spill coffee on the street. Muni had served San Francisco residents reasonably well for more than one hundred years. The cars were small but better than BART trains, which had mostly filthy seats. He maneuvered his way into a Muni car and found a place to stand near the door. The train started moving.

On his left, a big poster was pasted on the train's vinyl interior, a very attractive poster indeed. The California Academy of Arts invited students to apply for modeling and acting programs. He caught sight of a young, attractive brunette in his peripheral vision. She held the handrail steady and stared at the poster for a minute. Then, she balanced her standing position by pressing her toes on the train's wobbly floor and took a picture of the poster using her Samsung Galaxy phone.

He smiled at her. She smiled back.

"I studied there." He pointed at the poster. "It's a good school. It made me what I am today."

"Cool. Are you an actor?" the brunette asked.

"No. I am a photographer. Also, a casting agent."

The girl's eyes opened wide.

He wanted to keep the momentum going. "I help young actors get in front of casting directors."

"Wow, that is an interesting job!"

"Yeah, it is. Stressful as well." He reached inside his jacket and pulled out a well-designed business card. "My name is George Williams. Call me if you want me to help you get into college or if you want to model. You have a gorgeous camera face!" He winked.

"Oh, really?" The girl blushed. She paused for a moment and shook his hand. "Mr. Williams! My name is Selena Perez. I am a senior in St. John. I would love to get into modeling, even just for one picture."

"Call me George. I'll take more than one picture." He winked again. "Hey, I have a Facebook fan page. You will find the URL on the back of my business card. Check it out! I have tons of likes!"

"Cool! I will!"

Muni came to stop with a screeching sound. Selena peered through the window to make sure it was her stop and said, "I have to go. See ya!"

George waved back. *Call me soon!*

❧

George got the call in less than eight hours. "Mr. Williams! This is Selena. I checked out your fan page. It's so cool, you know!"

He twisted his lips and half-smiled. *I know.* "Thanks, Selena. It's very kind of you to say that."

There was silence on the other side.

"Are you there, Selena?"

"Yeah. Sorry, I did not know how to say..." She struggled for words.

"It's okay. I know you want to model. That's your dream! Don't hesitate to say it loud. Am I correct?"

"Yes! Yes!" She giggled.

"Let me tell you something. I think you have a great talent. A Disney show's casting director is visiting the city next week. I can introduce you to her." George made sure that his voice sounded authentic.

"Oh, really?" Selena could not believe what she had just heard. "Thank you. You have no idea how much this means to me. I can swear right now. You are my savior!"

I am your god. I decide your fate.

"No worries, Selena. I will check my calendar and set up a time." George continued with a question, "I guess after school is the best time for you?"

"Yeah, that will work. When do we meet?"

"Hold on." George put the phone on mute and waited for a minute as if he were busy checking his calendar. "Okay, I can pick you up after school on Friday. I have a studio in Novato, in North Bay." He noticed hesitation on the other side. "I have all the equipment in the studio. It's much easier to do it there."

"Sure, sure," Selena said in a hurried voice. She did not want him to mistake her hesitation for lack of interest. "I'll see you on Friday. You know where St. John is, don't you?"

"Yep. I know. I'll be outside at three o'clock. I have a red BMW. You won't miss it."

"Thank you, Mr. Williams. I'm looking forward to it!"

Me too. George clicked the end button on the phone.

Chapter 27

It was four o'clock on Friday afternoon. It took them forty-five minutes to cross the Golden Gate Bridge with the traffic and to reach Novato, a town thirty miles north of San Francisco. Selena got out of the BMW and looked around. It was an old industrial neighborhood. The street was narrow and surrounded by grocery store warehouses and graffiti-splattered abandoned buildings.

"What is this place?" she asked. It certainly did not look like a place for studios.

"Looks can be deceiving! Don't be fooled by the filthy-looking neighborhood. This place is good for creativity. I have almost no disturbance in this area. And I get to look at San Pablo Bay from my window. I have owned this place for more than seven years now. Don't worry; you will love my studio. Come on!" George sounded enthusiastic.

Selena climbed the stairs slowly and followed George to the second level. "It does seem to be a quiet place." Selena did not really mind the dirty stairs and filthy handrails. She was going to be a star in a year or so.

"Yeah. I love this place. Like I said, it gives me a lot of creativity to work with."

She nodded. "All right. So, the awesome studio is right here?" She pointed at the door with the engraved sign *Evergreen Memories* and smiled like an innocent two-year-old.

"Yes, ma'am. Right behind this door!" He unlocked the door and let her in.

She could not tell whether it was an apartment or a studio or a hybrid. The place itself was quite large. It occupied the entire second level. On her left, she saw a big kitchen. The living room had apparently been converted into a studio with wall mirrors, tripods, vanity chairs, and multiple cameras. She suspected a bedroom behind the mirrored wall.

He bowed with a smile. "Welcome to the studio that is going to change your life!" Then, he pointed at the small red couch placed in the middle of the light reflectors, tripods, lens bags, and digital cameras. She smiled and sat down.

"What do you drink? Coke or juice?"

"No, thanks." She looked around. "You have a nice studio here. I love Canon!" she said, pointing at the Canon Mark III mounted on an aluminum tripod.

"You know about cameras! That's good," he said as he opened the refrigerator and grabbed an orange juice bottle. He poured the juice into a plastic cup and walked to Selena who sat nervously on the edge of the couch.

"It's just orange juice. Please take it." He touched her shoulder gently and handed her the cup. "It will help with the dehydration from all these reflectors. We have a lot of work to do!"

She thanked him and sipped the juice as she watched

him fiddling with a stereo system mounted on the wall. Katy Perry streamed through Bose speakers.

Halfway through the song, she felt dizzy and caught sight of George leaning against the kitchen wall, sipping Blue Moon beer and staring at her with a smirk on his face.

~

Three minutes later, George stashed the beer bottle in the trash can and walked over to the girl crouched horizontally on the couch. Then, he knelt down, gently ran his fingers through her hair, and kissed her. She looked deeply asleep. The date-rape drug he had mixed with the orange juice would keep her that way for at least another hour.

He put one hand below her neck and another under her thighs and lifted her. He carried her over slowly without hitting the wall, pushed the bedroom door shut using his right leg, and laid her down neatly on the king-size bed.

Then, he started to undress her.

Tap, tap, tap.

Someone knocked on the front door. He shook his head. *Get lost.* He ignored the knock, removed his shirt, and started to explore Selena.

The knock on the door grew louder.

He jumped off the bed, walked quickly to the door, and violently opened it. A man stood tall, adjusted his hat, and smiled at him. He wore a weird long red gown and thin shoes.

"Don't you have any manners?" George blurted out. "What the hell do you want?"

The man rubbed his chin. "Sorry to bother you, buddy. I

was walking to that building over there…" He pointed at the back of the warehouse building across the street. "I heard a guy screaming for help. Did you scream for help?"

"What?" George's eyes turned red. "Just get lost, okay? I am in the middle of something." He turned to quickly close the door behind him and jumped when the man kicked the door open.

"Middle of raping a schoolgirl?" He slowly walked toward George.

A chill went down George's spine. His mind went blank for a second. Then, he quickly ran toward the kitchen to grab the butcher knife. It was already too late.

As he ran, he felt a blow on his back just above his butt. He fell down, and his lips touched the carpet fiber. The man threw both his knees onto George's sacrum, the triangular bone just below his spine, and pushed his gun into the back of George's neck.

"Where is she? The girl you picked up from Saint John?"

George lifted his head off the carpet and turned to face the angry man. "What are you talking about? Who the hell are you?"

"Answer my question, asshole." He kept the gun steady in his left hand and used his right hand to push George's head into the carpet.

The carpet smelled like urine. George felt the carpet fiber in his nostrils. He quickly moved his hip up in an effort to destabilize the man. It didn't work.

The man threw his right elbow onto George's head to land a painful blow.

George screamed. He badly wanted to get up. The

man's knees kept him from moving his hips and legs. His hands were stretched out on the carpet, almost touching the kitchen counter. All he could see was the carpet and a distant view of the oven door.

"Okay, I'll tell you. Let me get up."

Silence. The gun stayed in position as if the man waited to hear more.

"Listen, the girl wanted a photo shoot, okay? She left already. She should be in San Francisco by now."

The man removed his gun from George's neck and shoved it inside his robe. His knees stayed in position. He quickly knelt down a little, let his right arm slide around George's neck, and lifted his face up. "One more lie and I will snap your neck in a second. Got it?"

George's heart raced. He choked when the grip on his neck was tightened. He pushed his hands into the carpet in an effort to get up.

"Don't even try."

"The girl is in the room." George's voice was garbled.

"Is she alive?" The grip was tightened further.

"Yes."

Harrison let his grip loosen and used his left hand to keep George's face on the carpet.

"Don't move," he ordered.

Then, he slowly lifted his knees off, extended both his legs quickly backward, brought his hands to the sides of George's body, and pushed himself up swiftly. He stood a few inches behind George's shoes and looked around quickly.

The kitchen area was filthy. The living room was a different story with neatly arranged cameras and tripods.

He pointed his gun at George. "Slowly roll over and face me. Don't get up," he said in a stern voice.

George rolled over, faced the ceiling, and let his arms stretch out. His fingers trembled. He tried to hide his fear and sniffled. "The girl wanted to be here, okay? I didn't do anything. Trust me."

He stared at him as if he were studying every word George muttered.

"Who the fuck are you?" George immediately realized it was not a good thing to say to a man with a gun.

Harrison quickly pressed his right shoe hard onto George's left heel. The pain was unbearable. George flapped his hands on the carpet and tried to get up.

Harrison waved his gun to direct George to stay on the carpet.

"I ask the questions. You answer me. That's how it works. Do you understand?"

George nodded.

Next, Harrison removed his foot from George and slowly moved back. "Get up slowly. But don't stand up. I want you to crawl to the bedroom slowly."

George lifted his body, knelt down, and started crawling toward the bedroom. Harrison followed him, keeping a safe distance, and caught a glimpse of the girl on the bed. She looked like she was sleeping. But he knew what had happened.

"Okay, enough crawling. Stop right there and don't move." Harrison scanned the room. There was a large king-sized bed surrounded by beer bottles and trash cans. The curtains were closed over the glass door on the left. To his right was a bathroom and a walk-in closet.

He kept an eye on George, who looked like a dog facing the wall, walked around the bed, and checked the girl's pulse. "What did you give her?"

"Scopolamine."

Date-rape drug. He nodded and looked around. The bedroom smelled like a chemical laboratory.

George kept his crawling posture, turned his head to the left, and stared at Harrison. "Who are you, man? You have the girl. Take her and get out of here."

Harrison didn't say a word. He stood still as if he were thinking about what to do with George.

"You can't treat me like a dog." Infuriated, George pushed his hands off the carpet and stood. "If you want to kill me, go ahead."

George quickly lurched toward Harrison and extended his right leg in an effort to kick Harrison in the groin.

Harrison remained calm and gently moved sideways, letting George's leg pass by on his right. Before George realized what had happened, Harrison acted with lightning speed, grabbed his leg, and twisted it hard.

George screamed and fell on his hands. His face was a few inches away from the carpet. His right leg experienced excruciating pain as his left knee hit the floor hard. The man did not let go of the leg. George jerked like a fish thrown on hot sand. "Stop, stop, please stop!"

Harrison kept the pressure on as he watched George crying. "What is that smell? Chemical?" He raised a quizzical eyebrow.

George nodded. "It's just the chemical to develop films," he mumbled. "I am a photographer."

"Oh really? What kind of chemical?" Harrison applied more pressure.

George screamed louder. "Okay, okay! It's–It's to melt the body."

Melt the body.

"Where do you keep the chemical?"

"It's in the closet there. Please stop!" he screamed.

Harrison twisted his leg and snapped it. He ignored his screams and went to the walk-in closet, which looked like a high school chemistry lab. Bottles were labeled and arranged neatly on multiple shelves. A full row of bottles carried the label "Sulfuric Acid." *Bastard.*

He emerged from the closet and stared at George, who leaned against the wall and sobbed.

"How many girls have you killed?" He tried hard to control his emotions.

"I don't know." George avoided his eyes. "I am not lying, man. I really don't know. I don't want to kill these girls. It's just—I just can't control it."

"I can cure that disease."

George looked up. "Who are you, man? Why are you here? How do you know about this girl?"

"You are a Curious George, aren't you? Tell you what… Whatever goes around comes around. Do you know that?" Harrison paused. "You want to know who I am? I'm the guy who tracks assholes like you wandering around high schools. I have nothing else to do. I go around schools every day and watch for perverts like you. The moment I saw you outside Saint John, I knew you were trouble. I saw you sitting in your BMW, biting your nails constantly. You kept looking at the rearview mirror. I knew you were up to something."

He waved his gun at George. "Get up slowly and walk to the bathroom. Don't do anything stupid. I have no mercy for you."

As instructed, George slowly got up and walked toward the bathroom. He slightly turned to his right and switched on the lights.

Harrison scanned the bathroom. It looked much bigger with all the lights on above the giant-sized mirror. The twelve-foot-long bathroom had three big sinks on the left. The white bathtub, turned into a charcoal color, looked deeper than normal. The blue-colored walls looked ugly with graffiti scattered all over.

"Okay, keep your right hand on the mirror. Use your left hand to open that cabinet." Harrison pointed to the cabinet under the sink closer to the tub. George followed the order and looked up to meet Harrison's gaze. "Pull that bin out."

He pulled the Rubbermaid plastic storage bin out to the porcelain-tiled floor. Human bones were stacked neatly in the bin. Harrison jarred his teeth. "That's what I thought. Do you have more bins in these cabinets?" He waved his gun at the other two cabinets under the sinks.

George nodded.

The next second, George felt pain in his stomach and heard the shot. Then, there was one more shot. He clutched his stomach and fell on the tiled floor. Then, he smelled Harrison's boot, which gave the lethal blow to his nose.

Harrison shoved his gun behind his back. He knelt down, removed the phone from George's pants, and placed it on the countertop. Then he lifted George from the floor, using his gloved hands, and threw him inside the tub as if throwing a piece of dirt into the garbage can.

He ran to the living room, grabbed the Mark III camera, rushed back to the bathroom, and took multiple snapshots of George lying in the bathtub. He placed the camera on the bathroom countertop. Then, he quickly walked to the walk-in closet next door and strapped the gas mask on before grabbing two bottles of sulfuric acid. The mask smelled like cow dung. He wiped the dirty goggles before entering the bathroom.

He stared at the man inside the bathtub for a second and shook his head as if he just remembered something. He bent down, removed George's clothes, and threw them on the porcelain floor. Then, he slowly poured the acid into the tub as if he were pouring beer into a tall glass. He took more snapshots of George as the bubbles started penetrating his body. He let the camera sit on the countertop and pulled out the bone-filled bins from under the sinks. He grabbed the phone lying on the countertop, switched off the lights, and closed the bathroom door behind him.

The girl slept like a baby without understanding what was going on around her. The stench of sulfuric acid would soon occupy the bedroom. He removed the bed sheet and wrapped it around the girl. Then, he lifted her and carried her to the couch in the living room. He slowly let the girl down to rest on the couch before removing the gas mask. He walked across the living room and opened the large glass door facing the San Pablo Bay.

He took a deep breath and stared at the blue sky for a minute. Then, he called 911.

He threw the phone on the dining table and walked toward the front door. He stopped and shook his head as he looked at the gas mask lying on the carpet. Leaving DNA at the crime scene was the last thing he wanted to do. He grabbed the gas mask, opened the front door, and rushed out.

Harrison drove a few blocks down and waited at the corner of Stinger Lane. It took six minutes to hear the police sirens. He sighed and drove toward the Route 101 South freeway ramp. He had saved a beautiful jasmine garland from a sadistic monkey. His mind was peaceful now.

Chapter 28

Theaker looked at Samantha who was covering her nose. "Is this toxic?" she asked.

"The odor? Maybe. Sulfuric acid can be really nasty. Why don't you wait in the living room? I will be there in a few minutes." He grabbed the camera from the bathroom countertop and handed it to Samantha. "See what you can find in this. The killer purposely exhibited all these things for us to see," he pointed at the bones neatly stacked in the plastic storage bins arranged on the floor.

An acidic burn inched up in Samantha's throat. She sighed, exited the bathroom, and turned left toward the kitchen. She sat on the chair next to the dining table, pushed the menu button on the camera, and viewed the pictures one by one. *Horrible.* She felt like she was going to throw up. She placed the camera on the table and walked toward the red couch placed in the middle of the living room.

Large mirrors mounted on the wall and the bright lights mounted above the mirrors made the living room appear much bigger than it was.

She knelt down and ran her gloved fingers through the fabric of the cream linen couch. The fabric felt like velvet. She spotted yellow stains at the edge of the couch and a plastic cup on the carpet. She grabbed the plastic cup and turned to see Agent Theaker on her left.

"I think we should send it to forensic. The killer's fingerprints may be here." She pointed at the cup.

"Good point... This is your first crime scene. You don't seem very nervous. That's good!"

"The girl is alive and the bad guy is dead. I'm glad it turned out ok. Are we going to interview the girl? Can I come with you?"

Theaker noticed the rush of curiosity on her face. "Okay. The girl had a really bad day. I talked to Novato Chief. The girl doesn't remember anything about what happened after she had drunk the orange juice. Possibly a drug dose."

"Was the girl conscious when the cops arrived here?"

"No. She was deeply asleep and was covered by a bed sheet."

Samantha listened to the sound of wind coming through the balcony door. "I think the killer covered her with the bed sheet before calling 911."

Theaker raised his eyebrows. "You think he's some kind of savior. Right?"

Samantha shook her head. "I don't know. I'm just thinking," she pointed at the wall of the bedroom. "Mattress in the bedroom is missing the bed sheet. I suspect that the killer covered the girl with the bed sheet and moved her from the bedroom to the couch. We may get some clues from the bed sheet. His fingerprints may be there. Think about this... When you carry a girl from the bedroom to the living room, say for about thirty feet, your dress will rub with the girl's dress and her hair." She held her elbows as if she was carrying a toddler. "Is it possible that the fabric fiber loosened from your dress would be found on the bed sheet? Is it possible that you would leave some evidence without even knowing it?"

"Possible. But, it's a long shot. We may find the cotton fiber only if the victim struggled. Based on your theory, I don't think that happened here."

Samantha stared at the couch for a moment before speaking. "How about the pool of blood on the carpet in the bedroom? It looks like there was a fight. The killer might have lost some blood as well, right? We can get the DNA from the blood, right?" Her eyes widened.

Theaker nodded. "We will try that. Did you find anything useful in the camera?"

"Yes. I did," she said as she grabbed the camera from the dining table. "I think you should see this."

She pushed the menu button and scrolled through pictures. A pretty girl smiled. She lost the smile in the next picture. She lost her life in the following picture. The pattern was repeated for five more girls.

Theaker shook his head in disbelief. "It's a souvenir for the pervert." He took a deep breath. "We have a hard job of calling the parents of these girls with a bad news. At least now, they will have closure."

"There is really no closure when you lose your child."

Samantha stared at the LCD screen of the camera.

"Say that again?"

"Sorry, did I say something wrong?"

"No, no. Just repeat what you said before."

"There is really no closure when you lose your child?"

"Yes. That one." Theaker nodded. "If we work on a theory that someone, who lost his child, is doing all these killings... is it for closure or is it for something else? If I lose my child to a kidnapper and if I really lose my mind, I will go after the kidnapper. Maybe his family. But, why would I chase and kill all the pedophiles? Do I want to be a hero? or is it because I'm insane?"

"None of the above." Samantha looked at his eyes. "Like I said before, I think that the killer wants to send a message to all the pedophiles. It's a warning. *I am coming after you.*"

"Talking about warnings... I don't see *stay away from little girls* here? Well, the pervert is dissolved in sulfuric acid anyway." Theaker answered his own question.

"Agent Theaker!" Theaker looked up and saw an officer waving at him. "We have a witness here. Alejandro Salazar." The officer pointed at a man standing next to the main door. "He saw someone leaving the building few minutes before we arrived. Chief had already talked to him. I thought you may be interested in talking to him."

Theaker looked at the man. He was big, about six feet, dressed casually in an open-necked shirt and uniform short. He looked about thirty or forty. "What kind of smell it is? Is it a meth lab or something?" He covered his nose.

"You don't want to know. Let's go downstairs." Theaker signaled Samantha to follow him.

Samantha gently placed the camera on the dining table and walked fast to catch up with Theaker.

As they descended the wooden staircase to the ground level, Theaker introduced himself and Samantha to the man.

Alejandro stood still for a second and stared at the FBI badge on Theaker's coat. "I saw a weird guy leaving this building around five o'clock. Ten minutes later, I saw the cops coming in."

"Why did you say the guy was weird?"

"Well, he wore a long gown. Kinda funny. Looked like my wife's bathrobe!"

Theaker stood on the curb and scanned the road. He felt the light breeze waft across his face.

Samantha's eyes were fixated on Alejandro who crossed his hands over the chest and leaned against the cream colored wall. "You mentioned a bathrobe. Was he fully covered with that dress? Top to bottom?"

"Yeah, something like that."

"What color was it?"

"The dress? It was red. It went down to his ankle."

"Was he barefooted?"

"No. The guy had a black hat, long red gown, small shoes, and a helmet." He grinned.

"Helmet?" Theaker asked.

"Yeah. The guy carried the helmet in his hand before jumping into his SUV. Who needs a helmet when you drive a car?" Alejandro shook his head as he smiled.

"Are you sure it was a helmet? motorcycle helmet? or a

bike helmet?" Samantha asked.

Alejandro shrugged. "I don't know. It was black. It looked a little different than a motorcycle helmet."

Samantha thought for a moment. She pulled up her iPhone and searched for an image. When the images had shown up, she showed the phone screen to Alejandro. "Did the helmet look like that?"

"Maybe... Yeah, it looked like that." He shifted his legs uneasily.

Samantha turned her gaze at Theaker. "It's a gas mask."

Theaker looked at Alejandro. "The car he was driving? You did say SUV, right?"

"Yes, sir. It was Honda SUV. Dark color. Black or dark blue. I was unloading boxes from the truck there." He pointed at the Safeway warehouse on the other side of the road. "I could not see the model."

"Did you see his face?"

"Not much. I saw his face from the side. He looked like an Asian."

Theaker walked over to Alejandro and shook his hand. "Thank you, Mr. Salazar. We will contact you if we need more information."

Samantha waited until Alejandro disappeared from her view. She looked at Theaker. "I think we're looking for a monk."

"Huh? A *Monk*?"

Samantha nodded. "Based on the description from the witness, it looks like it. The killer is methodical. I won't be surprised if he is a monk."

Theaker stared at the street light. "We're looking for a monk with a gun?"

"And a mission."

Chapter 29

Alameda de las Pulgas, often referred to as "The Alameda," ran from Menlo Park to San Mateo in California and covered two high schools and three elementary schools on its path. The drive on the road was full of surprises for the visitors. Blind curves and abrupt change in the number of lanes caused a good amount of stress. Students jamming the road right after school at three o'clock added more stress for the drivers.

However, there was no stress for Marco and Hector, who were trolling the street in their Ford Escape. For them, it was fun, pleasurable, hunting time.

Marco slowly drove the vehicle on Alameda as Hector scanned the crowd and looked for the perfect prey. Their vehicle inched closer to Carlmont High School.

Sara, Liam, and Divya came out of the school campus and jumped onto the pedestrian path to cross the street as soon as the walk signal lit up. Sara tried to adjust her backpack to reduce the pain on her back. It didn't work; the bag was heavy. The pillow-sized physics book on the left hand, and the laptop on the right hand didn't help much. Divya turned to her right and smiled at Sara. "Do you want me to hold your book?"

Sara shook her head. "No, thanks. I'm going to get a rolling suitcase to carry all these things!"

Just then, she heard a loud creaking noise. A big fat silver metallic SUV stopped just a few inches from her. Her heart started pounding. The driver mouthed an apology. Divya grabbed her hand and walked fast to cross the street.

"Oh my God! Oh my God! I died there for a second, you know?" Sara shook her head in disbelief.

"These guys are assholes. No one respects the speed limit and traffic lights." Liam walked slowly along with the girls. "I am glad you are okay."

Divya nodded. "This happened a couple of times already. We should be careful next time. That stupid SUV looked so big at close range. That was evil."

Sara smiled nervously. "Someday, I will buy a bigger evil and crash that damned thing."

They giggled and turned left onto Carmelita Avenue. Liam waved good-bye and entered the third house on the right. "Stay safe, Sara!" He winked before disappearing into his house.

Sara slowly walked along with Divya. "Are you free tomorrow? Can we go to Stanford Mall?"

Divya narrowly avoided stepping in dog shit. "I can't look up straight in this street. These dogs mess it up all the time. The owners don't clean it up; the city doesn't clean it up."

Sara giggled. "You are OCD!"

"Yeah, yeah, whatever!"

"Okay. Answer my question. Stanford Mall? Tomorrow?"

"Stanford Mall sounds good. I'll need to sweet-talk my mom to get her to drop us there. It's so boring waiting for Caltrain." Divya referred to the Amtrak train service in California.

"Caltrain is boring? I see cute boys on the train all the time." Sara finally seemed to relax.

"They are serial killers; don't go near them." Divya's eyes widened as she presented her findings.

Sara laughed hard.

"Why are you laughing? Those boys are serial killers. They don't kill you physically but mentally." Divya looked serious.

"Whatever!" Sara dismissed her. They stopped at the stop sign, scanned the oncoming traffic, waited for the cars to stop, and then crossed the street. As they climbed up the street, which was slightly uphill, Divya turned to Sara. "Did you see that?"

"See what?"

"I saw that SUV, same color, on our left when we crossed, the one that almost hit you."

"Well, those people may be living here. All SUVs look the same anyway."

Divya shook her head. "Something is wrong."

"Oh man, you're scaring me, Divya. Let's move before I have another heart attack!"

They started walking fast and turned right onto

Huntington Lane. The big sign said "Welcome to Huntington Heights." Beautiful houses lined both sides of Huntington Lane. Divya stopped in front of a house on the right. "Call me tomorrow, okay?"

Sara nodded. "Bye."

"Hey, what's wrong?"

Sara shook her head. "Nah, nothing. I'm still in shock."

"Because of that freak? Don't worry. You want me to walk with you?"

"Nope. Bye!"

Divya stood there and watched Sara walking slowly uphill. She turned to the barking of her dog, Alex.

"Hey, did you miss me?" She grabbed the Maltese and entered the house.

∼

Sara liked climbing uphill. Going against gravity felt good. Her house was in a cul-de-sac. Her mother insisted on buying that house in spite of the obscene price tag. The evening breeze gently moved her hair. She shook her head slightly to move the hair out of her view. The street was quiet except for the sound of chirping.

When she was one hundred feet away from her house, she heard a loud creak on her left. Her heart thumped.

She turned to see the big fat silver metallic Ford Escape SUV with the backdoor slid open and a young man sitting in the backseat. He quickly grabbed her left hand and pulled her inside. Her heart started pounding hard. Instinctively, she dropped the book in her left hand and pushed him. Pushing him using her non-dominant hand did not work.

The man slapped her face, grabbed her hair, kicked her in the stomach, and pulled her in. Just before she realized what was going on and shouted for help, he closed the door. He slapped her again before wrapping duct tape across her mouth.

He tapped on the driver's seat and shouted, "Go! Go!"

He looked at Sara. Her eyes begged for mercy. He put his head down for a second and then placed duct tape over her eyes.

A few seconds later, the driver yelled at him, "Take her bag and throw it out there."

"Why? Why do you want to do that?"

"Damn it, just do it."

Hector pushed her head down, removed the backpack, opened the door quickly, and threw the bag out. Then, the Ford Escape sped up.

Divya heard Alex barking while she was gulping Sprite from the refrigerator.

"You mad dog! What now?" Divya marched toward the front door. Just then, she heard the creaking sound of the vehicle and looked through the window. *That SUV.*

She ran to the window on the right and looked to the left to get a glimpse of the vehicle. It was gone already, sputtering smoke. Then, she saw the pink backpack thrown on the front porch.

"Mom!" she screamed at the top of her lungs.

A middle-aged woman ran down from the kitchen. "Why are you shouting like that?" Then, she saw the horror on Divya's face. "What happened? What's wrong?"

"Sara…Sara's bag is there…out there. I just saw that van—"

"What van—"

"Mom, I'm scared. Hold on; let me call Sara." Divya punched the numbers and waited. Then, she heard the "Slow Down" ringtone coming from the other side of the door.

"Oh my God! Oh my God! Mom, call 911! Call Dad!" Divya walked back and forth. Her brown face darkened.

"Calm down, Divya. What happened?"

"Calm down?" She struggled to breathe before composing herself. Then, she dialed 911.

Chapter 30

Marco sped through stop signs on the small streets without stopping. He stopped for a second before merging with the traffic on the main road.

"Whoa, damn, can you slow down?" Hector shouted from the backseat.

Marco did not say a word. He stared straight at the road, the signals, the pedestrians, and the Safeway on the left. If he had focused on the rearview mirror, he would have noticed the Honda Odyssey that was following him and the monk who was squinting at his vehicle's tinted rear window.

Marco quickly scanned Ralston Avenue for any police cars. Nothing. The Belmont police station was only a few blocks away. It was a thrilling experience to kidnap from an area close to the police station. He crossed Ralston Avenue and drove uphill until he crossed Rolling Hills. A few minutes later, he turned left onto Fernwood Lane, drove for a few more minutes, and reached the house at the far end of Sylvester Lane.

He clicked the garage opener attached to the passenger-side sun visor before pulling the car into the garage.

"Man! What a ride!" Marco turned to the backseat and saw Hector staring at him.

"What?"

Hector put his head down. "Nothing."

"Okay, tell me. What's wrong?"

"It's her eyes. Those eyes really bothered me. She begged without saying a word. I can't look at her eyes."

"That's why you taped her eyes?"

Hector nodded. "I don't know if I can do this."

"Listen, *we* can do this. We always did this. We will always do this. There is nothing more fun than this. Remember, Bob is going to pay ten grand for this girl. We get to enjoy the girl and *also* get ten grand. Just like that! Come on; it's party time!"

Marco jumped out of the Ford Escape and came around to open the back door.

"We got a good catch, didn't we?" He looked at Sara, who sat still in the backseat.

Hector half-smiled.

Marco thought about asking for more money from Bob. "Okay, let's take her in. Grab her neck." He pulled Sara out of the seat and grabbed her legs. Hector held her neck and shoulders, slowly got out of the vehicle, and followed Marco.

Sara threw a kick vigorously, which landed on Marco's chin.

"Shit, what is wrong with you?" Marco put her legs

down, pulled a cigarette from his pants pocket, and lit it up. He inhaled for a second and then placed it on Sara's left leg. Her scream came through the duct tape.

"See...don't mess with me! Okay?" Marco carried her and signaled Hector to follow. He climbed the small steps in the corner of the garage and opened the door leading to the living room. He smelled menthol as he opened the door. Then, he slowly walked forward before coming to a full stop.

Two giant-sized creatures, one with a clean-shaven head and another with a receding hairline, curly mustache, and long beard sat on the couch in the living room. They looked like sumo wrestlers and fixed their gaze on Marco. The MAC-10 submachine guns in their hands were pointing straight at Marco's head.

Marco forced a smile onto his face. "Whoa...slow down, buddies. What are you doing here?" His blood pressure spiked because he knew the answer to his question.

The one with the clean-shaven head stood up and slowly walked toward Marco. He stomped on the hardwood floor with his big frame. Marco smelled margarita and pizza as the big guy came closer. He let go of Sara.

"Victor, I can explain." Marco rushed to speak before the big guy hit him, but he was late by a second.

Victor Anga punched Marco's nose hard. "Okay. *Now*, you can explain!" He smiled at Marco's bleeding nose. He turned to his left and saw Hector holding the blindfolded girl by her shoulders.

"Who is that?" Victor probed.

Hector didn't want to answer and looked at Marco, who was wiping his bleeding, jalapeno-shaped nose.

Marco raised his hand. "Can you just chill? Let me explain please."

Victor Anga nodded and carried his two hundred and sixty pounds back to the couch. He sat down next to Scott Kaleo, the guy with the curly mustache. Victor silently nodded to Scott.

Their grandparents had immigrated from the southern region of Tonga in the 1920s. They had been best friends since they were kicked out of high school for selling drugs in the classroom. They had become a little smarter since then, but their aggressiveness did not change a bit.

Marco signaled for Hector to drag Sara behind the couch and forced confidence into his face before sitting on the couch across from the sumo wrestlers.

"I apologize for the late payment. I did not mean to cheat you. How can I cheat you when you guys have MAC-10s and magnificent bodies?" Marco tried to smile but stopped after seeing the grim expressions on their faces.

"Okay. This is what happened. Somebody broke into our warehouse and stole the consignment we got from you last week." Marco noticed disbelief in Victor's face and continued, "Seriously. You have to trust me on this. You see the girl here." He pointed at the back of the couch. "She is going to get me ten grand. I will get the money tonight. I will pay your debt *tonight*. Just a few more hours."

Scott sniffed. "You're pimping now?"

Marco shrugged. "You can say that. For me, it's business. I do work, get the merchandise, and sell to interested buyers. You do the same thing. For you, it's drugs. For me, it's girls."

Victor rolled his fist and stomped on the couch. "You

have some nerve!" He raised his big eyebrows, showing scary reddish pupils. "I don't believe you. We are going to stay here until you give us the money."

"Not a problem." Marco turned to his brother, who looked terrified. "Take the girl upstairs and lock her up."

Hector shook his head. "I can't carry her up the stairs. I need your help."

Victor's voice stopped Marco as he got up. "*You* stay here. Scott will carry her with one hand!"

Scott pushed his right palm onto the couch and quickly rose. He walked around the couch, grabbed the girl using his right hand, placed her over his left shoulder, and started climbing the stairs.

Marco fixed his gaze on the monster sitting in front of him. He had to calm him down. "You know what? I made a mistake. But I want to make this up to you. Let's go upstairs and have a good time. You know what I'm talking about!" He winked.

Victor pointed his big index finger at Marco and laughed. "You are a real bastard!"

～

Marco waited until Victor reached the second level without breaking the wooden stairs. Then, he climbed two steps at a time, turned right to enter the master bedroom, and saw Scott standing next to the window. Sara was still on his left shoulder, struggling to get out of his clutches.

"Oh man…Why are you standing close to the window? No one should see the girl. Just put her down on the bed!" Marco shouted.

Scott grimaced and placed the girl on the bed. He looked

around the bedroom. The queen-sized bed was in the middle of the room, surrounded by plenty of wall paintings. The leather love seat was on the far right. Sunlight made the room look brighter than usual. He turned back and looked through the window. The backyard was full of junk with one rosebush in the corner. He looked over his shoulder and signaled Victor, who leaned on the wall closer to the door with the MAC-10 in his hand.

"Look at this. What a contradiction! These guys are trying to set up a garden in the middle of all the junk!" Scott laughed.

As both Victor and Scott enjoyed the view of the backyard, Marco gently removed the duct tape covering Sara's eyes.

Sara squinted. It took a few seconds for her to get accustomed to the bright sunlight in the room. She watched the man coming up from under the bed with double-braided nylon rope in his hand.

"Please let me go…"

Marco ignored her and tied Sara's hands to the bed's headboard.

Sara immediately rolled to her right and smashed her head into his nose in a bid to escape. Her head missed the target; instead, it hit his cheekbone.

Furious, Marco slapped her. "Listen, you can't get out of here now. We are going to play with you. You can go home after playtime. Do you understand?" He grabbed her hair and shook her head.

Sara nodded. Tears flowed.

"Okay, good girl!"

Marco removed the duct tape from her mouth and made an attempt to kiss her.

She spit in his face.

He jumped onto his knees. "You spit? I will teach you a lesson, bitch." He grabbed her head and banged it on the head frame. She felt the pain for a few seconds before losing consciousness.

Scott turned around after hearing the thudding sound on his right and watched the girl's head going down sideways. She stayed still. "Is she dead?" He grabbed her right hand and checked for a pulse.

"She's just unconscious. It's good in one way." A cruel smile formed on Marco's face. He jumped off the bed, closed the window curtains, and turned to Hector. "Go downstairs and get drinks for our friends."

Hector silently nodded and closed the door behind him as he walked out.

Hector shook his head as he climbed down the stairs. He had never liked Victor and Scott. He never liked dealing with drugs. But his brother was addicted to drugs and money. There was no stopping him.

His thought process came to a halt when he saw a tall man in a red monastic robe leaning on the wall, hands crossed over his chest, staring at him near the front door.

"What the hell? How did you get in? Who are you?" Hector stammered.

∼

Harrison quickly scanned the house. The large living room was littered with game consoles, whiskey bottles, rotten potato chips, and cigarette pockets. A dark stain-covered couch was placed closer to the fireplace. An expensive chandelier hung just above the coffee table. The glass sliding door next to the kitchen had shown part of the large backyard. The hardwood floor looked ugly with multiple black stains. The man frozen on the stairs was trembling and caused the aged wooden steps to shake.

"Where is the girl?" Harrison asked as he moved forward, closer to Hector, who watched in dismay.

Hector's face withered. "Huh?" The next second, he turned around and ran upstairs.

Harrison leaped forward and chased Hector, who quickly ran into the master bedroom.

Inside the bedroom, Victor and Scott turned their heads after hearing the violent banging of the door opening. Marco turned his attention away from Sara and grimaced at Hector, who was panting near the door.

"What is wrong with you, man? Why do you look like you just saw a ghost?" Marco asked as he watched Hector stammering to say something before running to the center of the bedroom. Then he spotted the tall man entering the room.

~

Harrison stepped inside the room, assessed the situation, and surveyed the faces of the four men. He made a mental note of the MAC-10 and quickly measured the distance between him and the gun. Then, he looked at the girl, with the torn green top, lying on the bed and the man who was about to undress her.

Years of training in the monastery had made Harrison a calm and composed person. However, his mind was enraged by what he had just witnessed.

On his left, two big guys smirked. Victor smiled at Scott and said, "Fucking monk!"

Scott leaned his big frame on the window, crossed his hairy long hands over his chest, and looked at Harrison. "You walked into the bedroom to beg *or* fuck?"

Victor laughed loudly as if he had just heard the joke of the year. His big belly swung up and down as he laughed. He threw a high five to Scott, to appreciate the rhyme. He pointed at the steel belt wrapped around the monk's waist. "Look at that! The *monk* needs a metal belt to keep his stupid gown from falling down!"

They laughed again.

Marco was not in a mood to appreciate the rhyme or the dry humor. He had been boiling with anger for the last twelve minutes, since he had to face the monsters with the MAC-10 in their hands. Now, he had to deal with a *monk*. He turned to Hector and shouted, "Why the hell did you bring this beggar here? Kick him out."

Hector shook his head as he moved back to the corner of the massive bedroom, across from the door. He looked around to see if he could grab a sharp object to throw at the man. Nothing.

Victor laughed again after watching the horror in Hector's face. He pointed his finger at Marco and said, "Man, your brother is a chicken!"

Marco gritted his teeth, rolled to his left, and jumped off the bed. He took quick stride toward the door, curled his right fingers into the palm, and used his knuckles to throw a punch at the monk.

Harrison quickly retracted his right leg from the door and used it to throw a round kick into Marco's chest.

Intense pressure on the chest and stomach caused Marco to destabilize. He burped as he fell hard on the floor.

Victor dropped his smile and tightened his grip on the MAC-10 while Scott fixed his gaze on the monk.

"What is that? Kung fu?" Scott mocked in a Chinese accent.

"No. *Krav maga* would be the right answer." Harrison moved forward toward the big guys, as he scanned to his right to make sure Marco and Hector stayed where they were.

Victor sensed the danger and held the gun steady. "Stay where you are. I will blow your head off!"

Harrison stood silent for a second. Then, he gently placed his right hand on his hip and quickly removed the shiny steel belt from his waist and uncoiled it.

In a second, the steel belt rapidly morphed into a long, flexible curling sword composed of six steel blades, each about sixteen feet long. Harrison wielded the sword and spun it as he moved forward toward Victor, who took three seconds to realize what was going on.

Harrison moved fast and whipped the sword across Victor's right hand. The sharp steel blade cut through Victor's flesh right below the cobra tattoo on his biceps and made him drop the gun.

In about eight seconds, the blades cut through Victor's entire body. He screamed with pain.

Harrison kept swinging the sword as he took a few steps backward and scanned his right side. Marco stood up and moved his right leg backward, apparently preparing to attack Harrison on his side. Hector leaned on the wall and watched in horror.

Harrison scanned to his left and kept an eye on the open door as he kept swinging the curly sword.

Victor fell on the hardwood floor on his big belly, which created a sound like a metal rod hitting a wooden drum. Blood gurgled from the side of his neck. His eyes widened in horror when he spotted his amputated right hand lying in the pool of blood.

Scott recovered from the shock, quickly fetched the MAC-10 that lay on the floor, and leaped forward with rage. He started firing at the monk, who rapidly spun to avoid the fire path.

Harrison heard bullets flying dangerously close to his right ear. He immediately sat on the floor on his left palm, extended his right leg for support, and swung the blades rapidly to his right. Multiple blades sliced through Scott's legs before he fell down on his face.

Harrison quickly stood up and continued to whip the blades to slice through Scott's shoulder and neck.

He moved to his side as he kept swinging the steel blades vigorously.

Marco moved backward and stopped as he hit the wall. Just then, he noticed Hector sliding down the wall and onto the floor, clutching a bullet-ridden chest. The MAC-10's stream of bullets had found a home in Hector's body.

Marco threw a fist into the wall and shouted, "Who are you, man? Just stop it. My brother is shot."

Harrison stopped spinning the blades, looked at the

girl for a second, and faced Marco, who continued to talk, "Listen—take the girl. Take whatever you want. Call an ambulance. My brother is shot. Don't do anything stupid, okay?"

Harrison twisted his lips as he coiled the long steel sword into a belt. "Don't do anything stupid? *You're* telling me?" In a blink, he leaped forward and threw a round kick into Marco's stomach, which pushed him closer to the wall.

In a split second, Harrison pushed his right arm hard into Marco's throat.

Marco choked and closed his eyes as his head banged on the wall behind him. He stammered. "Okay, okay, we made a mistake. Okay? Just call the cops. Don't kill me."

"I am *the* cop." Harrison paused for a second. "I am *the* judge. Get it?" He pushed the arm further.

Marco struggled to speak. "We were asked to kidnap the girls. It's not our fault."

Harrison loosened the grip a little. "Who asked you to kidnap her?"

"His name is Bob. That's all I know. I met him in a bar in Half Moon Bay. I am just a handler. He has many handlers to kidnap girls. I don't know what he does with these girls. Please trust me on this. I am deep in debt. I needed to pay off those guys." Marco pointed at the fallen sumo wrestlers.

"How do you plan to hand over this girl to *Bob*? Will he come here today?"

"No. I don't even know his number. He calls my cell and gives me the location. We go and drop the girl. That's how it works."

"What was your last drop-off point?"

Marco thought for a second. "San Mateo Fairgrounds. It changes every time."

"How many girls have you dropped off so far?"

Marco quickly spoke. "Just one. This will be the second girl."

"I don't believe that. Tell me the truth. You were monitoring the girls. I was monitoring you scumbags. The way you took this girl today, it did not appear like an amateur job. Tell me the truth. How many girls have you sold to that bastard?"

"Just one. Seriously man…" Marco begged.

Hector applied pressure to his chest, moved his back against the wall, and stretched his legs as he struggled to speak. "There was another girl—last year." He closed his eyes and put his head down. Fear of death engulfed him. "Just tell him, Marco." Tears dripped from his eyes.

"How old was she?" Harrison tightened his grip.

"Five." Marco's voice was adenoidal.

Harrison felt the pressure in his sinuses. He closed his eyes for a second, sniffled, and asked, "Where is she?"

"We buried her in the backyard. She tried to escape—" Marco gasped.

Harrison applied pressure aggressively until Marco stopped resisting. Then, he wrapped his right arm around Marco's neck, snapped it, and pushed the dead body down onto the floor.

He moved quickly, checked the pulse of the girl, and then walked toward Hector, who was already dead.

Chapter 31

Ackerman and Walker held the guns steady and combed through the living room and kitchen. Ackerman spotted a submachine gun on the couch and signaled Walker to check out the second level. When Walker stormed through the master bedroom door on the right, he saw the guy staring at him with dead eyes and a bleeding chest. He turned to the left. Two big guys lay semi-naked and dead in a pool of blood. His mind reached the possibility of a gang war when he saw the cobra and dragon tattoos on the big arms of both fellows—until he spotted the unconscious girl on the bed. She was wrapped up in a green comforter. On her right, there was graffiti on the wall. Two words were written with smudged big red letters.

"STAY AWAY."

Red paint, maybe blood, dripped down the wall. He held the gun steady in his right hand and slowly moved closer to the girl. He scanned the room one more time, leaned down, and checked her pulse.

He rubbed his nose and raised his brow after seeing the

laceration on the girl's wrists. He called the dispatcher to confirm the ambulance's ETA. As he ended the call with the dispatcher, Ackerman's voice came through his Bluetooth. "Walker, a guy is dead down here in the backyard."

"Stay there. I see three dead bodies here. The girl is alive, but not conscious. I'll come down."

Walker scanned the room one more time. He noticed the window broken behind the bed and leaned forward into the window. He could see Ackerman's shaved head facing the ground. In front of him, a body was lying on the ground. It was not really a body; there was no head. A headless, handless torso had been thrown fifteen feet down.

He quickly moved out of the room and checked the other rooms on the second level. There was no one. He heard the loud ambulance sirens. He ran downstairs, briefed the ambulance personnel about the girl upstairs, and then walked across the living room to reach the door opening to the backyard.

Ackerman turned around. "It's quite a scene here. This guy is cut into pieces and scattered around the backyard." He pointed at the left corner. "Look. There are two hands and…" He paused and pointed to the right corner. "The legs are lying there."

"Barbaric," Walker murmured.

Ackerman rubbed his temple. "It's not just that. This guy was pushed from that window." He pointed at the bedroom window upstairs. "Look here, all glass pieces." Now, he pointed at the bloody path on the ground. "The guy was pushed down from there, dragged down this way, and cut into pieces."

He looked over the fence surrounding the backyard.

"We need to talk to the neighbors. I would be surprised if no one saw this butcher cutting people into pieces."

Walker nodded. "Hmm, not sure what happened." He pointed to the body pieces lying on the ground. "We need to connect these pieces and find out what the hell happened in this place. Three dead guys upstairs. One guy down here in pieces. A girl up there...none of this makes sense."

"Lieutenant, the FBI is here." A voice came from behind.

Ackerman turned around and saw Detective Aguinaldo standing near the door.

"Really? That was quick." He pointed at the bloody path on the ground. "Get forensics here."

Detective Aguinaldo nodded and leaned against the wall to make way for Ackerman to move inside. Ackerman quickly jumped into the living room and noticed emergency personnel carrying the girl on the stretcher. The oxygen mask had hidden most of her bruised face.

He climbed upstairs and entered the large bedroom swamped with cops and FBI agents. A man in his mid forties kept taking photographs. Two men and a young woman stood near the broken window and faced the door. One of them smiled at Ackerman, moved closer, and extended his arm.

"Good to see you, Lieutenant." Agent Theaker shook Ackerman's hands and pointed to the other man. "This is Agent Jones." Then, he pointed to the woman. "This is Samantha Cruz. She's an intern. Berkeley student. Smart kid."

Ackerman smiled slightly and shook hands with both of them. "I am Lieutenant Ackerman." He added, "I worked with Agent Theaker on a couple of cases." Then, he turned to Theaker and said, "This is going to be a memorable one."

"Why is that?"

"There are body pieces in the backyard. The killer used the dead guy's phone and called 911. He left a message in a robotic voice and said that the high school girl kidnapped from Belmont could be found here. We got here in seven minutes." He paused. "I am super glad that the girl is alive."

Theaker nodded. "Did you say body *pieces*?"

"Yes, sir! The killer is some kind of a butcher." His gaze fixed on the graffiti on the wall. "*Stay Away*? Is this the same guy?"

Theaker nodded. "Yes, apparently. This could be a copycat. There are a couple of differences between this and the previous murders. In the previous instances, the killer used permanent marker and wrote it on the foreheads of the victims. This one—" He pointed to the graffiti and continued, "It could be blood or paint. We don't know. We need to wait for the lab results. One more thing—a different kind of weapon was used here." He dropped to his knees and pointed to the big guys lying dead on the floor.

"Look at all these cuts. Whatever that weapon is, it sliced through the skin, like a knife on a banana." Jones and Ackerman joined Theaker, looked at the multiple slices on Scott's torso, and shook their heads.

Samantha broke the silence. "I think I know what the weapon is."

Theaker looked up.

Samantha sat on her knees to level up with her new boss. "I think it's a *urumi*."

"Urumi? What kind of name is that?" Ackerman asked.

"It is a weapon used by warriors in the southern part of India in the olden times, a few hundred years ago. I have seen people using this weapon. It's effective to handle multiple opponents."

"Where did you see this weapon?" Jones asked.

"In a place called Kerala, in South India. I went there when I was junior in high school. I volunteered for a nonprofit to teach schoolchildren in rural areas. We were there for the entire summer. Local people taught us their martial arts, *Kalaripayattu*. It was like a much older version of kung fu. Anyways, the urumi is a weapon with multiple steel blades. It's a long sword made of flexible steel, sharp enough to cut into flesh, but flexible enough to be rolled into a tight coil." She pointed to the slicing in Scott's stomach. "The skin is sliced simultaneously. Probably six blades together. Look at how deep the wounds are. I am pretty sure it's a urumi or a weapon like that."

"You think the killer came from India or got trained in India?" Ackerman looked bewildered.

Theaker answered before Samantha could say a word. "Let's not speculate anything. Let's see what the forensics say about the weapon." He looked at Ackerman and said, "Okay, let's go and look at the body *pieces* you talked about."

Chapter 32

Theaker scanned the backyard, which was basically a junkyard except for a rosebush in the far-right corner. Two chairs and one desk were in the middle of the garden. Tons of beer bottles had been thrown under the desk. The place was filthy except for the rosebush.

A rosebush.

The plant's beauty was overshadowed by two amputated arms, which were neatly placed on the ground in a V-shape. Theaker walked closer to the plant and looked at the lifeless hands lying on the soil.

Jones joined Theaker. "Got something?"

Theaker shook his head. "I don't know. Most of the body pieces were scattered there…" He pointed to the place where Marco's head had been abandoned. "That's where the killer pushed that guy through the window. However, the killer placed the dead guy's hands *here* for a reason. See…the fingers are pointing to the plant."

He sat on his knees. Jones knelt down across from

Theaker and sifted through the soil with his left hand. "Something is buried underneath. Look at the heaped pattern here. There is more than just a rosebush here." He stood up. "I think we should dig under this plant."

～

Walker looked around when he heard a ringtone. "Shake Your Whammy Fanny." He walked closer to the headless torso from where the ringtone originated. He removed the phone from the dead man's pants pocket.

The caller ID flashed "Unknown."

His gloved finger touched the answer button. "Hello?"

"Marco?" It was an older voice on the other side.

Marco?

"Marco is busy. He is all worked up and torn into pieces right now. Who are you?" Walker waited for the answer but heard only the sound of rapid, shallow breaths on the other side before the call was disconnected.

～

On the other side of the call, Bob McFarlane looked at the man in the wheelchair. The man was bulky and wore blue jeans and a green-striped half-sleeve shirt. He wiped the sweat from the bridge of his nose, adjusted his eyeglasses, and asked, "What happened, Bob?"

Bob scratched his head and sighed. "I'm not sure, Thomas. Marco is not there. Someone else answered. Does not look good. Something is wrong." He arched his brows. "Once I get ahold of this bastard, I am going to kill him."

"I want my princess." Thomas tightly gripped the arms of the wheelchair and stared at the blue sky through the window. "It's supposed to be my birthday. I want my princess."

~

It was six o'clock in the evening. Samantha was exhausted after witnessing the unearthing of a human skull under the rosebush. Part of her wanted to cry. Part of her wanted to look tough.

Jones slowly walked toward her. "You are getting a hell of an experience during your internship." He pointed to the fallen rosebush. "Looking at the skull, it looks like a small child was buried there."

Her heart sank. "Maybe the cops should dig up the entire backyard?"

"Yeah, maybe. We don't know how many children these monsters killed." Jones sighed.

Samantha nodded with sadness. "Do you remember our discussion during my interview? I still think that whoever killed these monsters is a good guy. If not for him, these monsters would have killed even more children."

Jones stared at Samantha for a moment. "The *killer* is a killer. Don't praise him as some kind of Robin Hood. We can't let people take the law into their own hands. It's our job to catch the killer before he butchers even more people. You can't let your emotions cloud your judgment. If you are going to work in FBI, having good judgment is very critical. It may very well save your life someday."

Samantha crossed her arms, folded her lips and nodded.

Chapter 33

Laura read what she wrote for the fourth time.

I am a single woman, 32, looking for a Valentine! Must be real and not looking just for a good time. I am real and waiting! I can't host. Hope you can. Serious real people only. Send me your favorite flower in the subject line so I know you're real!!

She felt clever for adding the requirement of a favorite flower in the subject line. She had gotten tons of spam the last time she posted the ad in the women-seeking-men section of the online classifieds website. She hoped it would be less spammy this time. As she clicked the post button on the screen, her blood pressure rose a little.

The computer time showed 10:00 p.m. when she heard the knock at the door. Angel peeked her head through the door.

"Mom, I feel sleepy. I will finish the homework tomorrow. Good night!"

Laura got up, hugged Angel tightly, and kissed her on

the forehead.

"Are you still searching for a job, Mom?"

"Yeah, sending ten résumés a day. Nothing's happened so far."

"Well, good night." Angel closed the door behind her.

Laura waited for a few minutes and switched the browser tab to see if there had been any response to her online posting. Nothing. She sighed and browsed through the job ads.

Ten minutes later, when she checked the email program, an email was waiting to be opened. The email subject said, "Rose for you!"

Interesting. She opened the email.

> I loved the way you wrote. I am looking for someone to marry. I love kids. But due to an injury, I can't have kids. If you have children, that would be awesome. If not, that's okay too. But I want to tell you this beforehand. Check out my picture and let me know if you want to hook up tomorrow.

Laura opened the attachment to see the picture, a good-looking guy. Her heart started racing a little bit. She wondered how old he was.

"How old are you? I like your picture. Here is mine." Laura composed the email and sent it away.

A reply popped up in a minute. "I'm thirty-two. Just your age, and just your type."

"Nice! I would love to meet you tomorrow. Where do you live?"

"Awesome! I live in Fremont. But I can meet you in a

Starbucks closer to you. Hey, are you okay with the kids' stuff?"

"Yeah. Don't worry about it. I have a daughter. I do not plan to have any more kids. So, trust me; it doesn't bother me. I am okay."

"Daughter?! Cool. I love daughters. Are you still married? I do not want an affair, you know what I mean?"

"LOL. No worries. I am single, divorced."

"Single is good. I do not want your husband to shoot me, you know :-) How old is your daughter? Is she going to school?"

"She is eight. My ex moved to Australia. He won't shoot you. No worries!!!"

Laura thought about adding multiple smileys at the end but left it with exclamation marks. She clicked the send button and waited.

"Australia?!! That's nice. I have never been married. I was worried about commitment. Now, I am kind of settled in the business. It's time for me to start a family."

Starting a family. Just what she wanted.

"I think I already like you very much. We have a good vibe. Let's meet at 11:00 a.m. tomorrow. Okay?"

"You got it, dear!"

∼

Laura felt anxious as she gazed at the long line forming in Starbucks. She wondered how many of those women waiting in the line were single with children. *It's not easy, girl.*

She looked around and saw no one closely resembling

the man she was expecting. She got the coffee, walked slowly looking for a place, and then found a table in the corner, near the window, with just two chairs.

As she looked through the window, she saw a guy emerging from a pickup truck parked closer to the side entrance of the coffee shop. Her heart started beating a little faster. *Is he the one?* He looked more charming than he looked in the picture. Laura put her head down and continued to sip the coffee. She did not want to look desperate.

"You must be Laura!"

Laura looked up and smiled at the young man pulling the chair out in front of her.

"Yep. I am the one. You Gilbert?"

"Yes, ma'am!"

Laura looked around after shaking his hands. "So, how are you? You want coffee or something?"

"Nah. I am not a coffee drinker. I use Starbucks as a free meeting place. You see the people standing in the long line there? They take care of feeding Starbucks employees. I'm just a guy who takes advantage of them!"

Laura did not get the joke. But she liked the way he smiled. *Lovely.*

He was a fast talker. He talked about his electrical wiring business, how he lost both his parents in a car accident, and his passion for mountain hiking—all within seven minutes.

"Have you tried mountain hiking, Laura?"

She slowly shook her head. "No, I am not much of an adventurous person. What if I slip down the hill or hurt my ankle? I feel much safer on a treadmill."

"You know what? Mountain hiking is no different than putting some incline on your treadmill! I plan to hike this weekend in Sierra. Come with me; it will be fun. I will carry you on my shoulders if you are afraid." He winked.

She blushed. "Hmm…that would be nice!"

∾

"The madman is on a killing spree." Theaker tapped the table with a pencil.

Samantha looked through the conference room window. "Super Bowl 50" was displayed on the billboard mounted above the building next to UN Plaza. Super bowl mania swept through the city.

She stood up, adjusted her blazer, and walked over to a whiteboard. She pointed at the red circles on the map that was pasted on the board.

"Thousand Oaks to Belmont. All the *stay away* murders happened only in California."

Jones shook his head. "That's a big assumption. This guy is a psycho. He might have murdered people in other states without writing graffiti on them."

Samantha twisted her necklace.

"Let's hear what she has to say," Theaker said.

Samantha continued. "The killer is methodical. He had a chance to kill many others, but he didn't. He targeted only pedophiles. The killer broke into the homes of the victims. He had opportunities to steal valuables, but he didn't. He used a voice changer to call 911 after almost every murder. He wanted us to know that the abducted girls were alive… We don't have any tangible leads so far. We have only one witness who had seen the killer. As per the witness, the killer is a monk. Why would a monk kill the pedophiles? What does he get out of it? What is the motivation of the killer? Let's play a couple of what-if scenarios. What if the killer is someone who lost a child in the past few years? What if the killer is a lunatic disguised as a monk?"

Jones waved his hand. "This is not academia. We don't have a lot of time to go through all these scenarios. We have to find this guy before he dismembers more bodies."

"Okay. How about starting with the first scenario and narrow it down even further? The killer wants to send a message *stay away from little girls*. The message focuses on the girls. So, let's assume that the killer lost his daughter to a pedophile. Now...we need to define a timeframe and a geographical region. What if the killer is the guy who lost his daughter to a pedophile in California in the past five years?"

"How did you come up with *five* years? Why not ten years?" Jones frowned.

"I think we should define a strategy with a reasonable number. Once the strategy is in place, we can tweak the number if we don't find the suspect in the given timeframe."

"Your selection criteria would give us at least one hundred suspects. That's impossible to work with. We need to narrow that down." Theaker continued to tap the table with his pencil.

"Hmm...How about a guy who has nothing to lose?"

Theaker stopped tapping. "What do you mean?"

"Someone who lost his only child. Maybe someone who lost everyone in his family."

"*That* should bring down the number quite a bit." Theaker nodded. Then, he looked at Jones. "Samantha does not have access to Sentinel," referring to internal computer system, "Please work with Samantha and get the names of all possible suspects. Then, we should interview each guy on the list."

Jones rolled his eyes. "I think we are wasting time. Samantha has no experience in the field. We should act on specific leads instead of—"

Theaker raised his hand. "She has a fresh, clear mind. I think she is onto something. Let's try it."

∿

"You have a date, Mom?"

Laura looked up and saw the twinkle in Angel's mischievous eyes. "No! We are just friends. We will hang out for a day, that's all."

"Who are you kidding, Mom? I haven't seen you this excited for some time." Angel cocked her head to the side and smiled.

Laura got up and gave Angel a tight hug. "I can't hide anything from you! You are just too smart, aren't you?"

"Yep. I am. So, tell me. You have a date, Mom?"

"Yeah, yeah, yeah!" Laura nodded her head. "It's a date! Gilbert seems to be a nice guy. I hope he will stay that way, you know."

Angel giggled. "Yeah, I hope so. I can't let bad guys stay here. I will kick them out!"

Laura paused for a moment and realized her little girl had grown. "You are brave, Angel. I like that."

"I know." Angel hugged her.

~

Laura waited near the front door when Gilbert pulled up in his pickup truck in reverse. She walked closer to the driver-side door and waited for Gilbert to get out.

He gave her a big grin. "Ready for hiking, ma'am?"

"Yes, sir."

"Okay, I think we should start moving. Did you pack? Should I help?" he asked.

"I have just one bag. We are coming back tomorrow, right?"

"Yep. Is there anyone else living with you? Just you and your daughter, right?" He gently grabbed her hand as she opened the front door.

"Yes. It's just me and Angel. My sister lives in Morgan Hill. She will be here by noon to take Angel to her home."

They walked inside the house. The medium-sized living room was cluttered with toys, video games, water paint, and small chairs. Angel sat on the couch with her hands on her right cheek and stared at the man entering the house.

"You must be Angel! I'm Gilbert."

"Hi." Angel got up, smiled, and shook his hand.

"You really look like an angel. Your mom gave you an appropriate name."

"Actually, her dad gave her that name. She was born five years after our marriage," Laura said.

"I am sure that the man had good sense for names. What grade is she in?"

Laura noticed he kept staring at Angel. *What is that look?*

She sighed. "I think we should get moving."

"Sierra can wait. I want to know more about Angel," he said as he lowered himself onto the couch, next to Angel.

Laura crossed her arms over her chest and watched Angel moving to her right, a few inches away from Gilbert to avoid him.

He giggled, slid himself to his right, and moved closer to Angel.

"Mom, I want to watch TV." Angel was about to cry.

"Gilbert, give her some time to know you. Let's get moving now."

He looked up and smiled. Then, he puts his finger to his mouth as if to signal "Don't say anything." Then, he grabbed Angel's left hand. "See...You look so beautiful. Your skin is so soft." He rubbed her hand slowly.

Angel looked uncomfortable.

Laura stepped forward.

"What grade are you in, *baby*?" He grinned.

Angel quickly closed her nose. "You smell so bad. Don't come too close to me."

His face turned red. "I am going to be your stepfather. You need to learn some manners, young lady."

Angel gasped and looked at her mother, who moved closer and pointed her right index finger at Gilbert.

"*Stepfather?* What is wrong with all you men? I think you should get out of my house now."

"Whoa, whoa, whoa. Slow down. All I am asking is what grade she is in! You are making a big deal of it!" He turned to Angel. "Okay, Angel. Tell me; what grade are you in?" His smirk remained.

Laura said sternly, "Angel, go back to your room. I have to talk to Gilbert."

Angel got up and walked slowly toward her room.

"Oh, man! You are scaring that little girl, Laura. Look at her. How can you yell at that little angel?"

Angel stopped walking, turned around, and looked at Laura.

"Goddamn it, just go to your room!" Laura screamed. Angel ran to her room. Laura's blood started to boil. "You son of a bitch, get out, right now!"

He did not seem to be angry. Instead, he smiled.

"What is that fucking smirk? Just get out."

"You really don't get. Do you?" He slowly got up as he shoved his hand into his pants pocket.

"What—" Laura stopped when she saw the gun in his hand. The next thing she knew there was a blow to her head with the back of the gun and a voice from afar.

"I did not come here to take *you*, bitch."

Gilbert opened the door with a gun in his hand. Angel screamed.

"Shut up. I will kill you if you scream again."

"I want to see my mom." Angel started crying.

"Your mom is dead—"

Angel screamed louder and ran toward the door.

Gilbert grabbed her hair with his left hand and slapped her face with his right hand three times. She stopped crying and dropped her face into his hand. He dropped his hold on her hair and watched her falling down on the carpet.

"Oh shit."

His phone rang as he checked her pulse. He slid his hand quickly into his right pants pocket, and pressed the side button to ignore the call. Then, he ran to the truck, lifted the thirty-one-foot-long wheeled ice chest and rolled that down into the house. He lifted Angel from the carpet and positioned her inside the ice chest before closing it. As he rolled the ice chest toward the entrance, he paused for a moment to look at Laura. Then, he pulled the trigger.

~

About twenty minutes later, Gilbert took a left turn before Hayward Memorial Park and drove straight for three minutes. Then, he took a sharp left to enter a narrow road leading to small house surrounded by redwood trees. He parked the truck in front of the lonely house and jumped out.

His phone rang again. Now, he answered it. "Yes, Bob. You will get the girl tomorrow." He closed his eyes and took a deep breath after ending the call. He remembered his grandma as he smelled the eucalyptus aroma in the air. He had spent most of his nights in his grandparents' house after getting beaten up in the middle of the fights between his parents.

He came back to the present moment and remembered the girl. He pulled the ice chest down and rolled it toward the front door.

The front door was wide open. He remembered locking

it before heading out. He pulled his gun out and held it in his right hand as he rolled the ice chest wheeler using his left hand.

As he stepped into the house, he saw an Asian man in a Raiders hat and weird red dress sitting on the edge of the L-shaped dark-gray couch and staring at him, a MAC-10 in his hand.

"What the—" Gilbert raised his gun.

"Don't even think about it. If you make even the slightest move, I will blow your head off. Leave that box there, and walk *slowly* toward me." The man stood up and waved the MAC-10.

Gilbert let go of the ice chest without looking at it and inched forward. His mind was occupied with strategies to knock down the man standing in front of him. The door was still open. For a moment, he thought of crouching quickly, dodging the bullets, and running toward the back door.

"Okay. Enough. Stop right there," the man ordered.

Harrison glanced at the ice chest. "What is in there—"

Gilbert charged forward to attack him in the face.

Harrison moved slightly to his right and let Gilbert's arm pass by. Then, he used his left leg to kick hard at the side of Gilbert's left knee.

Gilbert lost his balance and fell on his right side on the couch. Harrison aimed his gun at Gilbert's knees and fired one bullet into each knee. The suppressor in the submachine gun silenced the shots.

Gilbert screamed.

"Is it painful? How many little girls screamed like this? Do you have a count of how many lives you destroyed?"

Gilbert leaned his back on the couch. "Who are you, man? What are you talking about?" Blood started pouring from his knees.

"What is in that box?" Harrison pointed his piercing eyes at the wheeler before turning them to Gilbert.

"That's none of your business."

"Really?"

Gilbert closed his eyes without saying a word.

"You stay right there. Make another move, I will put a bullet in your head." Harrison kept the aim steady on Gilbert's forehead as he started moving slowly backward. As he got closer to the wheeler, he slammed his right leg on the front door to close it.

He scanned around and looked at the couch for a brief moment. Then, he held the gun steady in his left hand, opened the ice chest with his right hand, and found the girl in a fetal position.

"You motherfucker." Harrison leaped forward and slammed the gun into the side of his head. Gilbert instantly fell down on the floor.

Harrison pressed his shoe hard on Gilbert's left knee. "Is that girl alive?"

"Yes! Yes!" he screamed.

"What did you do to her?" Harrison lifted the pressure from his knee.

Gilbert crawled backward on the floor and leaned against the dirty couch full of cigarette burns. "Nothing. I just brought her here. Who are you, man?"

"Who am I? The correct question is: *Who are you?* Are you a human being or an animal? You went to prison for molesting your stepdaughter. Even the prison time did not teach you a lesson. You stuffed a small girl into a box?" Harrison spit in his face.

Gilbert looked up and stared at the MAC-10, which was pointed right at his nose. "Listen, I made a mistake. Okay? Just call the cops, okay?"

"You look like a well-built guy. Why don't you find a woman and marry? If you want to have sex with someone, why not try someone your age, moron?"

Gilbert stared at him without saying a word. He stretched his injured legs, his hands on the floor.

Harrison continued, "Oh, I know why. Because you are a coward. You can't go after women your age because they will kick your ass. You can show your courage only to young children, is that it?"

Gilbert raised his right middle finger above his head. "Fuck you!"

"No. Fuck this." Harrison took a machete he had hidden behind his shirt and swung it in a semicircular motion. Gilbert's right wrist was cut, and his hand fell to the floor.

"These hands will never touch another innocent girl. Do you understand?"

"You cut my hand off!" Gilbert screamed. He sobbed in pain and disbelief. "You are barbaric!"

Harrison waited for a minute; he wanted Gilbert to feel pain before dying. Then, he threw the machete onto the couch, lifted the MAC-10, aimed it just below Gilbert's belly, and shot multiple rounds.

Then, he threw the gun on Gilbert's dead body and looked around. It was eleven o'clock, but there was not much light inside because of the trees in the backyard. He walked back to the ice chest and lifted Angel, who was in a deep sleep. He carried her slowly to the right corner of the couch and let her lie down there.

He walked to the kitchen, grabbed a water bottle from the refrigerator, and sprinkled the water on Angel's face. After a minute, she slowly woke up.

As soon as she opened her eyes, she screamed.

Harrison took a step back. "It's okay. Don't cry. I am a good guy. I'm like your father. The bad guy is dead. Look down on the floor. See? He is dead." He pointed at the dead guy.

Angel looked down at the man lying in the pool of blood and screamed even louder. "I want my mom!"

"Okay, okay. The cops are coming now. They will take you to your mom. The bad guy is dead. Don't worry!"

Angel sobbed as she looked at the dead man. "He said that my mom is dead. I want my mom…"

His heart sank. "You know what? That crook lied to you. You will see your mom soon." He wiped the tears off her face. "Listen, I want you to be brave and talk to the cops about what happened. Okay?"

Angel nodded.

He sat on his knees and searched for a phone. He found one in Gilbert's left pocket and handed it over to Angel. He said, "Call 911. Tell them what happened, okay?"

Angel nodded and dialed 911.

"Hello, my name in Angel. I am scared. Somebody hit my mom and took me to his house."

"I am here to help you. My name is Diana. What is your name again, sweetie?" the operator asked.

"Angel."

"Good. Where are you, Angel?"

"My mom's boyfriend hit her and took me to his house. Can you please come here? I am so scared."

"Do you know where you are now?"

Angel put the phone slightly down on her right shoulder and whispered to Harrison, "She wants the address."

Harrison adored her voice without showing any emotion. "Just hold on." He signaled to her to wait and rummaged through the paper stack on the coffee table on his right, between the couch and love seat. He found a utility bill, handed it to Angel, and circled the address using his finger.

Angel nodded and read the address to the operator. A few minutes later, she pressed the end button on the phone and looked up. "She said that cops are coming in a few minutes."

"That's good. You will be fine." Harrison stepped forward and put his palm on Angel's forehead. "God bless you, child! I am going to go. The cops will take you to your mom."

"Can you stay with me please? I don't want to sit here with that dead man." Her hands trembled as she pointed at Gilbert.

"That's a good point. Let's go outside."

They walked briskly and opened the front door. There was total silence. Harrison pointed at a small wooden bench on the front porch. "Please sit there. The cops will come soon. I can't answer their questions. I can't let them see me." He rubbed his temple as if he just remembered something. "Listen…The cops will ask you about me. Just tell them you didn't see my face very well. Can you do that please?"

Angel nodded. "Who are you?"

He struggled for words. "I–I am a father who lost his daughter, an angel like you, to one of these monsters." He took a deep breath. "I need to leave now."

"Can you stay with me *please*?" she asked innocently.

"I want to, but I can't stay here. I can't deal with the cops right now. I will hide behind that tree." He pointed to the cluster of redwood trees on his right. "And I'll keep an eye on you until the cops come. Then, I will go. Okay?"

"Okay." She nodded hesitantly and looked down at her toes. After a second, she looked up and said, "Thank you."

Harrison smiled, waved, and walked quickly toward the woods. He hid behind a redwood tree and watched the road. A Mercedes passed by. Birds chirped. Harrison could hear only his breathing now. A minute passed. Then, he heard the sirens. He smiled and turned around to see Angel, who sat there on the bench with no emotion on her face. She placed her hands to her temples and stared directly at the trees. *She is really an angel. How she is going to live without her mother?* He felt a lump in his throat. The sirens grew louder. He moved to his left and started walking fast, real fast.

Chapter 34

The lonely house was not lonely anymore. Hayward Police officers, FBI agents, and forensic experts scattered around the house, inspecting every corner.

Gilbert had been dead for two hours now. Angel was taken to Kaiser Hospital in Hayward. Captain Kayla Mueller, an officer in the Investigations Operations of the Hayward Police Department, rubbed her temple as she fixed her gaze on the message written on Gilbert's chest. "Stay away from little girls."

Mueller turned to her right to catch the eyes of Theaker and Samantha. "I presume that the serial killer you are looking for did *this* as well?"

Theaker nodded. "It looks like it."

"Do you have any leads on the killer?"

"We have a list of suspects. We are getting closer to catching the killer."

Samantha asked, "Do we know anything about this

guy?"

"We do. His name is Gilbert. He is a registered sex offender. He served six years in San Antonio for molesting his stepdaughter. He moved here last year. He ran a contracting company and did some work for PG&E," Mueller said, referring to Pacific Gas and Electric Company. "This house belonged to his grandmother. She passed away three years ago."

Theaker knelt down and inspected the gunshot wounds on the dead man's knees and pelvis area. He cocked his head sideways before looking up. "We need to run ballistics. The shots are aggressive and deep. It looks like a *machine gun*. Maybe a MAC-10 or 11 or an MGP. Could be a gang."

Mueller shook her head. "No. There was only one killer. The girl said that a Japanese ninja killed him."

Theaker stood up. "The girl saw the killer? *Ninja?*"

Samantha turned quickly to face Mueller. "Ninja? Are you sure? He's not a monk?"

"Well, that's what the girl said. I think she's going through post-traumatic stress. She's been taken to Kaiser. Apparently, someone with a mask saved the girl and killed this guy Gilbert. The girl told me that he looked like a ninja. I'll interview her again after she recovers from the shock." Mueller continued, "The killer might have come here to kill Gilbert for some other reason. It could be a robbery. The entire house was ransacked when we reached here. The killer searched for something in his bedroom and here." Mueller pointed at the wall cabinet that held a sixty-inch Panasonic Viera.

"What did he search for? Do we know?" Samantha asked.

Mueller shook her head. "Not sure. All these drawers were open when we got here." She grabbed DVDs from the top drawer with her gloved hands. "These are all porn, in the worst possible, sickest way."

"I think that the killer left clues for us," Samantha said in a quiet voice.

"Well, there is more. I found all kinds of sick stuff in his bedroom. If we comb through this guy's computer, we may be able to find the killer's motives."

Theaker nodded and rubbed his chin. "We'll take care of the computer forensics... At least the girl is safe. Do the parents know?"

"The girl's parents are divorced. The father is in Australia. We're trying to get ahold of him. The mother was shot dead." Mueller shook her head in sadness. Then, she pointed at Gilbert. "This guy was the new boyfriend. He killed the mother and took the girl here."

Theaker was visibly angry. "He probably befriended the mom to reach the child. The good news is that the girl is safe and the bad guy is dead. The bad news is that there is a serial killer out there, and…we don't know what he is up to."

≈

Bob McFarlane stared at the glass pieces scattered on the floor. Then, he looked up apologetically to the man in the wheelchair.

"Sorry, Thomas. I did not mean to rattle you. I should have knocked on the door."

Thomas Erskine removed his Gucci eyeglasses, rubbed his eyes hard, and placed the dark plastic frames gently on the bridge of his nose. "It's all right, Bob. I just slept for a second. When I heard your voice, I thought it was a dream." He chuckled as he moved his motorized wheelchair in reverse.

Bob grabbed the broom from the corner and swept the glass pieces holding drops of orange juice into the dustpan. As he stepped out of the large bedroom, he said, "The lunch is ready. I will wait for you in the dining room." Then, he left without waiting for a reply.

Thomas stared at the girl on the bed. Her eyes were closed, and her right leg was chained to the wooden frame of the bed. He adjusted his eyeglasses, maneuvered the joystick of the wheelchair to get closer to the bed. Then, he kissed the girl. "My princess!"

Tears flowed from the girl's eyes.

He ignored the tears and steered the wheelchair out of the bedroom.

Right in front of him was the backside of a large leather couch. Brown leather love seats occupied both sides of the couch, which faced the seventy-inch LED television on the wall. A Bose sound bar was placed strategically below the television to maximize the surround-sound effect. The KRON 4 news channel showed the weather report.

The kitchen to his right looked small compared to the living room. He stopped the wheelchair closer to the mahogany dining table and took a small turn and then reversed to have a good view through the window.

The barn behind the house looked beautiful through the shiny aluminum window. He pictured his grandfather standing in the entrance of the barn and handing him the Arabian horse. *The horse.* He sighed and looked deeply sad.

"What is wrong, Thomas?" Bob asked as he spread the mustard on the bread.

"Nothing. Just thought about Grandpa."

"He was a good man. I would have been a dead man a long time ago if not for him." He stared at the life-size portrait hanging on the wall behind the dining chair.

Thomas gave a wry smile, grabbed the bottle on the table, and gulped the water quickly. Most of the water dripped onto his shirt through his curling lips.

Bob grabbed the towel hanging on his shoulder and gently blotted the shirt.

"Sorry, Bob! I feel terrible when I trouble you." Thomas looked at Bob's eyes.

"Don't mention it! I am grateful to your family." Bob took the sandwich plate and placed it on the edge of the table.

Thomas stared at the television screen as he munched the sandwich. The analog clock hanging near the front entrance had shown two o'clock when the afternoon news started on KRON 4.

The news anchor, an Asian woman in her late twenties, smiled at the teleprompter.

"Good afternoon. Headline news for today. The eight-year-old girl kidnapped in Fremont earlier today was found within a few hours in Hayward. Her kidnapper was killed."

Thomas stopped eating and looked at Bob, who had already moved to the living room. He stood behind the sofa and stared at the woman on the television.

The news anchor provided more details after the teaser

headline. "An eight-year-old girl kidnapped from her home this morning in Fremont was found within two hours in Hayward. The girl's identity has not been released. Gilbert Hibbs, the alleged kidnapper, was found dead in his home when Hayward Police responded to a 911 call. The girl is safe and is being treated for trauma. A police department spokesperson told our correspondent that there will be a press conference at five o'clock this evening."

"Gilbert Hibbs? Is he the same guy?" Thomas asked.

"Yes. He was our handler." Bob pushed his tongue behind his upper teeth and twisted his lips. He appeared especially evil while doing so. He continued, "These bastards are good for nothing. They keep screwing up. I will take care of it from now on. I will get the girls." He looked very determined.

Chapter 35

Maya McKenzie tried to focus on the teacher as she pushed her right palm into her cheek. Mr. White raised his hand and asked, "Who can help me to subtract twenty-one from one hundred?"

The third-grade class gasped.

Sheena, sitting in the first row said, "I know how to subtract 21 from 22." The class giggled.

"That was crazy." Maricel, who sat next to Maya, poked her tongue into her cheek.

Maya tried to focus on Mr. White, who turned to the board to explain the subtraction magic, but caught sight of Austin in her peripheral vision. He sneaked under his desk and pulled the curly long hair of Laura, who was sitting in the front row. Laura shrieked.

The entire class looked in the direction of the scream. Laura stood up. Tears fought to come out.

"What happened?" Mr. White seemed concerned.

"Someone pulled my hair from behind." Laura tried to control her tears to avoid embarrassment.

Mr. White walked toward the row behind Laura. He stared at three students sitting in the row. "Who did it?"

Austin posed like puppy lost in the carnival.

Maya stood up. "I saw it. It was Austin. He pulled Laura's hair. I saw it." She pointed at Austin.

Austin ground his teeth. "No! She is lying, Mr. White. I was just trying to subtract the numbers you gave. I did not move from my chair." He moved his gaze to Mr. White.

"That's good. Can you tell me what numbers I gave for subtraction?"

His mind went blank momentarily. "Hmm…forty-one from one hundred?"

The class laughed. Maya smiled a little and lowered herself into her seat.

Mr. White nodded. "You know what, Austin?" He stared at him for a few seconds. "I think we should call your parents and tell them about what you really do in this class. It's about time."

Austin forced a cough. "I have a bad cold. Sorry, Mr. White. I was not paying attention."

"I thought so. I want you to go to the nurse's office and wait there. Once you get the medicines for your cold, then you should stay in the detention room until five o'clock. Is that understood?"

Austin took his backpack, stared at Maya, and walked slowly out of the classroom.

Maya did not blink. She shrugged and looked at Mr.

White, who went back to the board.

~

When the final bell of the day rang at two forty-five in the afternoon, Maya got ready to go home. She gathered her books and pencil pouch and shoved it into the backpack. As she pulled and strapped on the backpack, Lisa stood next to her with a broad smile.

"Hey, can you come with me to the library? I need to drop this off," Lisa pointed at *Charlie and the Chocolate Factory*.

"I like *that book*! I want to be like Charlie one day! I want to visit and stay in the chocolate factory *for the whole day*!" Maya giggled, creating a tiny dimple at the corner of her mouth. "Okay, let's go!"

After Lisa dropped the book at the library next to the school office, both of them slowly walked toward the main entrance where parents lined up in their cars to pick up the students. Maya spotted Austin staring at her through the office room window. She looked away and kept walking.

Volunteers from fifth grade maintained order in the area closer to the main entrance and made sure that the cars kept moving. Lisa spotted her mother's car waiting at the end of the line and impatiently waited for the car to come closer to the designated pick-up spot. Cars moved slowly, and Lisa got her turn a minute later.

Maya stood still and watched Lisa's car disappearing from her view before she started walking toward Bellevue Street and turned left. As she adjusted her Power Puff Girls–themed backpack and walked on the pedestrian path leading to Bellevue Street, she remembered Austin staring at her through the office window. *Bully. I am not afraid of bullies.*

Austin had always been a bully. Maya had not liked him since preschool days. He somehow managed to get away with all the trouble he caused.

Maya walked for another seven minutes to reach the intersection of Humboldt and Poplar Avenues and waited for the walk signal. A long line of cars formed along Poplar Avenue, which ended with the freeway ramp leading to Route 101.

The walk signal turned green and beeped. She looked to her left to make sure cars were stopped, adjusted her backpack to ease some pain, and crossed the intersection before jumping onto the pedestrian path leading to her apartment complex, which was three more blocks away. She walked past a coffee shop on her right across the street. Then, she spotted a huge black van parked in a strange way on her side of the street, twenty feet away from where she was. An old man sitting in the driver seat projected his bald head out the window and smiled at her.

Who is that?

She looked down, moved to the far left of the pedestrian path, almost to the point of hitting the wire fence surrounding the nearby football field, increased her pace, and walked past the vehicle.

"Hi, there, is this Humboldt Street?"

Maya stopped and looked back in the direction of the croaked voice. The old man moved the van forward to get closer to where she stood.

She nodded.

"Good. I am going to Rockwood Elementary School to pick up my granddaughter. How do I go to the school?" He smiled warmly.

Maya felt at ease when she heard her school's name. She moved a little closer to the driver's-side door and pointed at the school playground. "That is the school play—"

In a split second, the man grabbed her shirt collar and backpack together and pulled her in through the driver's-side window.

Maya's eyes widened with sheer shock. The next second, her head hit the dashboard. The backpack felt heavier, and her head hurt badly. She bounced back and shouted, "Help! Help!"

The man rolled up the tinted window on his side and moved the vehicle quickly.

Maya swiftly moved, rolled down the passenger side window, and put her head out through it. "Help! Help!" She wanted to shout louder, but the panic made her voice nasal.

The man used his right hand to violently pull her into the passenger seat and slapped her. She fell on the floor mat. He drove the vehicle diagonally to merge into the traffic going toward Peninsula Avenue. Forty seconds later, he crossed the Peninsula intersection, where the traffic light had just changed to green, and turned right into a small lane. He stopped the vehicle in the middle of the street and pulled a white towel from his coat pocket.

He leaned down to reach Maya, who was shivering in fear on the floor mat, placed the towel over her nose, and pressed it for a few seconds. She tried to push his hands away but failed.

He quickly changed gears, drove forward, turned right, drove for another minute, and climbed the ramp leading to

Route 101 South.

~

Harrison noticed the black Escalade, parked illegally facing the flow of traffic across the street, as he walked out of the neighborhood coffee shop. He had observed the same black Escalade a few days earlier when it was parked *on the curb* near Rockwood Elementary. A big vehicle in such a small street was hard to miss.

His day got started just like every other day in the past eighteen months. He woke up at six and ran for an hour on the treadmill while he caught up on crime reports and news. Then, he meditated for an hour in front of the giant Buddha statue in the living room before spending twenty minutes planning the day and the schools to cover.

He placed the latte cup in the cup holder and clicked the play button on the small blue screen mounted below the air duct when he noticed the black Escalade had started moving. He watched the vehicle with curiosity and disgust and hoped that someday the driver would get a ticket for parking against the flow of traffic.

He wondered whether the arrogant driver was going to make a U-turn in the midst of oncoming traffic or jump across the street to merge with the moving traffic to Peninsula Avenue. Just then, he noticed a small girl peeking her head out through the window, waving her hand and yelling something.

What was that?

The girl disappeared in two seconds.

Harrison quickly started the engine and slammed the blue screen to stop the music.

Chapter 36

Harrison maintained a reasonable distance and followed the Escalade, which appeared more like a miniature elephant. He crossed the Peninsula Avenue intersection and watched the Escalade take a right turn at Bayswater Street. He moved further, turned right, and saw the Escalade stopped in the middle of the road. He parked on the right shoulder and waited for anyone to get out of the vehicle.

A few seconds later, the Escalade suddenly jerked and sped toward the stop sign. It then quickly took a right turn.

Harrison felt the tickling in his heart. He quickly moved to his left, ignored the honk from behind, drove straight, and turned right without stopping at the stop sign. He felt the sweat on his forehead and ignored it. The Escalade was one among many vehicles waiting to enter the freeway ramp. It took a slight left and climbed onto the Route 101 South freeway ramp. He followed it four cars behind.

The Escalade passed two exits on the freeway and took a right turn onto Route 92 West, leading to Half Moon Bay. Harrison quickly changed lanes and entered the Route 92

West ramp.

Originally called Spanishtown, the small town had been renamed Half Moon Bay in 1874. The town rested on the Pacific coast between forested hills and some of the most beautiful coastline in California.

The Escalade took a quick exit from 92 West and sped onto the Route 280 South freeway. He reached to his left and flipped a switch located just below the cruise control button. Police radio communication streamed through the Bose speakers. He switched between the California Highway Patrol and the San Mateo County law enforcement channels. There was no sign of any missing girls, *yet*.

After crossing the Canada Road exit, he jumped two lanes to the right. The Escalade was going at a steady speed on his left side now. The windows were heavily tinted. There was no sign of anyone.

The image of the innocent young girl yelling through the Escalade's window flashed through his mind.

Then, he remembered April.

Tell my dad.

He wiped the tears away and focused on the road ahead.

∼

Harrison slowed down after watching the Escalade flashing the right indicator and taking the Route 84 exit leading to Woodside. He followed the vehicle, keeping a reasonable distance and making sure not to give away his intent. That strategy worked for about seven minutes until the road became a single-lane road. Now, he was directly behind the Escalade. He maneuvered the vehicle to make space for some bicyclists who were heading toward the trail near Woodside Creek. Then, he watched the Escalade slowing down at the stop sign and turning right onto an unnamed, unpaved road.

Flat farmland covered both sides of the road. Poles carried aged electric wires above. Three minutes later, he passed the cattle farms on the right. The ranch house was visible in the distance. A big, faded sign on the cattle farm said, "Welcome to Erskine Ranch."

A few seconds later, the Escalade took a sharp right onto a narrow road leading to the ranch house. A medium-sized sign warned, "Private entrance—no through street. Dogs running freely."

Harrison drove straight without stopping. He adjusted the right-side mirror to watch the Black Escalade, which had entered the ranch house area surrounded by walnut trees.

A giant sign on some dry farmland to his left screamed, "No Water, No Jobs." He slowed down the Honda Odyssey and parked it under a redwood tree on his right.

He grabbed the binoculars, jumped out of the vehicle, and checked his surroundings—farmland, cattle farms, sagging electrical wires, and redwood trees. Big Basin Redwood Mountain was visible in the distance.

He adjusted the binocular strap around his neck and focused on the wooded complex. The strong odor of manure was in the air. Cows roamed around walnut and western juniper trees. He had a partial view of the house inside the compound.

He looked around. There was no other house in the vicinity, just the cattle farms and trees.

He grabbed his backpack and started walking toward the

house.

The road was quiet other than the noise his shoes were making crunching the dry leaves on the side of the road. He stopped behind a walnut tree, gently pressed the binoculars to his eyes, and surveyed the area.

The Escalade was parked closer to the entrance of the house. A rusted boat trailer had been abandoned near where the Escalade was. Eight brown pillars held the front porch steady. The single-floor house could easily be forty-eight feet wide and sixty feet long. A big dish antenna protruded from the center of the saddle roof, which was decorated with Spanish-inspired brownish-red tiles. Down below, Mediterranean-style arched windows added beauty to the side wall, which was painted ivory.

He held the binoculars steady and focused on the wooden structure behind the house—a horse barn. The barn was big enough to accommodate at least ten horses.

He shifted his focus to the fenced area in front of the house. The fence enclosed a green garden and a big redwood tree, which spread its branches twenty feet wide. There was a paved driveway around the fence.

As he turned his gaze back to the house, Harrison noticed a tall old man coming out of it. He was at least six foot two with a long face and a flat nose. His eyes were deep and were showing signs of fatigue. Harrison figured he was around seventy years old. He had no facial hair and a clean-shaved head.

He walked around the Escalade and opened the passenger-side door. He reached inside and emerged with a girl over his shoulder.

The girl appeared to be sleeping. But her hands hung

lifeless and her neck was rigid. The tall man could very well be her grandfather. But he did not act like a grandpa. He was very mechanical in the way he carried the girl inside. He carried her as if he were carrying a birch log and disappeared into the house.

Harrison shoved the binoculars into his backpack and inched forward to the side of the house. As he moved forward, he used his left hand to adjust the steel belt wrapped over the robe around his waist.

Now, he stood in the corner of the farmhouse and looked around before taking quick strides to reach the driver's-side door of the Escalade. He peeked through the window. No one was inside. There was no child seat, no booster seat, no candy wrappers, and no cereal scattered inside of the vehicle. Instead, the back seats were occupied by kitchen bags, plastic gasoline cans, a cordless drill, and a portable saw.

The mission-style arched front door of the house was visible through the vehicle's tinted window. Two small arched windows were on the both sides of the front door. The front door was left open, but there was no sign of the old man or the girl.

He moved between the trailer and the Escalade, crouched, and quickly ran toward the side of the house. He crouched again to avoid the arched windows on the side wall before briskly walking toward the back of the house. He stopped and slowly poked his head around the corner to study the situation behind the house. No one was in the vicinity. The back of the house had similar architecture to the front.

The place was quiet except for the calming sound of the wind and the occasional dripping of water from the red-tiled roof.

Then, the heart-chilling scream of a young girl came from inside the barn. "Go away! Leave me alone!"

Harrison felt a thousand small needles poking his temple. He was ready to storm into the barn but stopped when the barn's wooden door was violently opened as if someone had kicked it from the inside.

A bald, bulky man on a motorized wheelchair emerged out of the barn. The man wore thick glasses, a torn T-shirt, and khaki shorts. He closed the barn door, turned around in his wheelchair, and drove straight into the main house through the back door, which was symmetrically aligned with the barn door.

Harrison waited for a minute and then quickly ran to the right side of the barn. It was a typical horse barn with four small square-shaped glass windows on each side. He peeked through the first window on his right. It was dark. He waited for a few seconds to get his eyes accustomed to the darkness. No horses were inside the stall and there was no smell of hay, animals, or grain.

Then, he heard sobbing coming from his left. He moved to the next window.

He gasped when he saw two girls lying on the floor, inside the stall, with their legs chained. The tail end of the rusted chain was attached to the small steel structure in the corner of the stall.

He looked closely. A thin black cloth was wrapped around the girls' eyes. The stall was about six by four, with cracked boards. Two feed buckets were placed in the corner.

He gently knocked on the window to see if the girls would respond. Silence. Nothing happened.

He slowly moved to the next window and peeked inside. There was another stall with a split door. No one was inside. *Wait.* A girl, may be seven years old, wearing a pink gown, had curled herself up tight in the right corner. Her legs were chained; a moistened black ribbon covered her eyes. She placed her head between her knees, sobbing and panting.

He gently knocked on the window. The girl looked up.

Before he could say a word to the girl, he felt an intense pain in his peroneus longus, the muscle area just below the knee. He jerked off from the window to face the eyes of an enraged pit bull, which grabbed his right leg with its sharp teeth. He quickly pulled his right leg inward and then extended it rapidly up in the air, throwing the nasty-looking dog on its head on the rocky ground.

The pit bull squealed.

He looked down and saw the bleeding muscle and torn robe. The pain was irritating but bearable.

He looked up when he heard the barking and prepared himself for the onslaught of another pit bull, which emerged from the back door of the house and charged like a cheetah. It covered twelve feet in three seconds and tried to land on his stomach with a vengeance. He quickly positioned himself for the frontal assault. He tilted his left foot sideways and threw a kick.

The dog went up in the air and landed on the back wall of the house. It did not give up. The tenacious dog got up, barked loudly, and came straight at his face this time.

Harrison lifted his left heel, pulled a tiny blade from the back of the shoe, and aimed it at the neck of the charging pit bull. The cyanide-soaked blade's tip took the life of the pit bull in about five seconds.

"Who the hell are you?" The tall man stood near the rear entrance of the house with a shotgun in hand. He looked at the dogs lying on the ground. "What did you do to my boys?"

Harrison stood silent.

"Who the hell are you?" Bob McFarlane repeated the question.

"I am a tourist. I am lost." Harrison adjusted his hat and looked at the tall man's prodding eyes. "I am from Texas. I stay in Woodside, at my friend's place. I lost my GPS. My phone battery is gone. I got a flat tire. So many bad things in one day! I saw this house and came here to see if I could borrow your phone to make a call," he continued with a sorrowful face, "I am really sorry for the dog."

Bob waved his gun and signaled Harrison to come closer. Harrison lifted his arms in surrender and moved slowly as he kept an eye on Bob's hand movements.

Bob stopped Harrison at a safe distance and spoke in croaky voice. "Don't lie to me. Who are you? Monk? What are you doing here?"

Harrison kept his arms up, shrugged his shoulders to adjust the weight of the backpack, and quickly lifted his left leg to land a blow on Bob's groin.

The next second, he felt the pain in his left leg and fell on the floor. He looked up to his right to see the man in the wheelchair with a baseball bat in his hands. The man quickly sent another blow, this time to Harrison's right leg.

Bob rushed forward and placed the shotgun to Harrison's forehead.

"Uncle Bob, just kill him already. He killed Roger!"

Thomas shouted in a high-pitched voice.

"Roger is dead?" Bob kept the gun steady.

"Yes. Roger is dead. Now, drag this guy inside. He is no tourist."

Bob signaled Harrison and watched him get up. He smirked when Harrison struggled to get up. He pushed the bayonet to Harrison's shoulder.

"Go in. You will never come out of this house. I will bury you next to Roger."

Chapter 37

Harrison felt more irritated by the howling of the man in the wheelchair than the bayonet pushing into his neck. As he was forced into the house through the back door, the first thing he spotted was the young girl wearing a blue-green shirt and blue skirt, tied up to a midcentury amaranth-red chair, next to the leather couch in the center of the living room. *Same girl.*

Bob pushed the bayonet into Harrison's neck and shouted, "Keep moving."

Harrison tolerated the discordant sound reverberating in his ears and looked over his right shoulder. The tall man was furious. Behind him, the man in the wheelchair stared at him with rage and fear. His eyes twitched constantly. Mucus flowed down from his nose. His fingers played a virtual piano to control his anxiety.

"What the hell are you looking at? Keep moving!" Bob kicked Harrison's bleeding leg from behind.

Harrison quickly lifted his left hand to slide the bayonet

down to his backpack. Once the bayonet was off his neck, he quickly folded his fist and launched his left palm forcibly under Bob's chin. The surprise blow made Bob lose his balance. Harrison used the small window of opportunity to quickly strike between Bob's legs.

Harrison jumped off the floor and used both his legs at the same time to kick Bob just below his knees. That made Bob's legs fly sideways out from under him.

Bob fired a shot aimlessly as he fell down along with the gun.

Harrison quickly retreated and came to a standing position, staring at the man, who sat holding his groin on the floor. The man's face showed the crushing pain he was suffering because of the impact of his nuts striking the floor so hard.

The girl screamed. Harrison turned around and put his finger to his mouth to signal her to keep quiet. She screamed again.

Harrison turned around, looked out the back door, and searched for the wheelchair. It was not there.

Harrison moved closer to the old man and pushed the shotgun away to his left. The gun bumped into the oven door and made a *clunk* sound.

He quickly scanned the area. There was a large kitchen on his left with a small bar table and a large-sized mahogany dining table on his right with six royal leather chairs. He counted three rooms behind the large couch in the living room. A giant-sized television hung on the wall on the other side of the living room. Between the couch and the television, the girl was tied to a chair with nylon ropes. One rope tied her hands and stomach to the upper part of the chair. Another rope tied both her legs to the chair's front legs. The girl was still screaming. He realized there was no point in asking her to be calm. He had to focus on the old man clutching his nuts on the floor. He also had to find the man in the wheelchair.

Bob gathered himself from the floor and inched his butt backward toward the wall. When he looked up, he met the avalanche of blades emerging from Harrison's hand and felt the blood coming out of his neck and left arm. He pushed his right palm to the ground, got up quickly, charged forward, and stopped when his right leg was cut off below the knee. He fell down in a pool of blood, just below the glass window facing the barn.

The six sharp steel blades in the weapon clinked with each other and produced a rhythmic jingling sound as Harrison stood still near the bar stool and pulled the weapon back toward him.

Bob looked up. "What did you do to me? Who are you?" He spat blood onto the marble floor.

"Someone who has been hurt by evils like you."

"I am no evil. I am a grateful man. Thomas is like my son. I wouldn't be alive today if not for his grandpa, Mr. Erskine." He caught his breath and pointed at the life-size portrait of an old man in his seventies wearing a charcoal suit riding an Arabian horse, which hung on the wall right behind the dining table.

Harrison stayed alert and let him continue talking.

"I was orphaned when I was fifteen. You have no idea what I went through. Mr. Erskine gave me a life. But…his entire family is gone except Thomas, poor boy." He sniffled. "Poor boy, he lost his parents when he was very young. Just like me." He stared at the portrait on the wall for a second before looking at Harrison. "You know what? All I ever wanted was to give a good life to Thomas."

Harrison arched his brows. "How? By locking up all those girls in that barn?" His blood pressure spiked as he spat the words.

Bob stared at the portrait again. "Just before Mr. Erskine died, he told me to do whatever was necessary to make Thomas happy. The boy wanted the girls to marry. He calls them *princess*. All I did was get them for him." He gazed at the portrait as if he were worshipping the man in it.

Harrison shook his head in disbelief. "Are you insane?"

"Thomas is still a boy. He wants to marry these girls, *all of them*, as a matter of fact. It's his legacy. It's my responsibility to help him. I owe it to this family."

Legacy.

"You are retarded. Did you ever think about these kids' parents? They are enduring an unbelievable hell on earth. Do you fucking realize that?"

Bob looked at Harrison's red eyes and smirked. "I don't even know who those people are. They can always have another child, you know." He shrugged. "If they are able to reproduce!"

Harrison was appalled to see the man had no remorse for what he had done. He sat on his left knee and placed his right knee on Bob's bleeding stomach.

"You have two seconds to live. Think of all the lives you have shattered." Then, Harrison quickly reached to the side of his robe, pulled out a small but sharp knife, pushed his left palm in a cup motion on Bob's chin, and sliced through the carotid artery in his neck.

Bob died a painful death. The house was quiet except for the sound of bubbling blood. He stared at Bob's dead eyes for a second, quickly got up, scanned the living room, and looked through the windows to watch for any signs of the other man. None.

The girl stopped screaming. Instead, she cocked her head sideways and silently watched him moving from the dining area to each room on her right.

Harrison checked the small room behind the dining area. There was a twin-size bed on the left and small desk near the window. Metal chains, nylon ropes, an aluminum ladder, and shovels were scattered on the floor. The walls were decorated with black-and-white portraits of the older Erskines. There was no sign of the wheelchair. He came out of the room and moved to his left as he kept scanning the living room for any danger.

He entered the next room. He felt like he had just entered a ToysRUs showroom. The marble floor was littered with toys—Barbie dolls, yellow Minion creatures, a pink-colored bird cage, and a giant doll of Queen Elsa. A pink-colored wall was covered by small stickers of Power Puff Girls, Barbies, and butterflies. There was no furniture. He saw no closets. Sunlight coming through the small window illuminated part of the room. There was no sign of the man or the wheelchair. He quickly got out.

When he entered the next room, which was much bigger than the other two rooms, he was shocked by what he saw.

A girl, in her early teens, leaned against the bed frame with a small pillow to support her head. Her left hand was chained to the steel frame. She was dressed like Rapunzel, a character in a German fairy tale—Rapunzel with a bruised face and innocent eyes that had lost all hope.

"Who are you?" she asked in a brittle voice.

He scanned the room without saying a word. He looked behind the door and checked the closets. There was a giant bed in the middle of the room with a helpless girl on top of it. The walls were decorated with cartoon characters—Mickey Mouse, Pinocchio, Ariel, and of course, Rapunzel.

A large wooden almirah, an ancient one, was on his left, right next to the bed. He quickly walked over and opened the door, hoping to find the man hiding in there. Instead, he found colorful costumes ranging from clown attire to a superman suit. He closed the door and looked at the girl, who was staring at him with fear.

"What is your name?"

"Teresa Goldberg." The girl's eyes moved in despair. "Are you going to hurt me too?"

He immediately remembered the Amber Alert he had seen a few weeks ago. "*Teresa*...I am sure your father will be so happy to see you!" he said in a low voice. "I will get you out of here. Don't worry. I am looking for the man in the wheelchair. Did he come here?"

She shook her head.

"Okay, just stay here. I will be back soon." He walked over to the door and turned back to look at her. "Don't worry, Teresa. You will be home soon. I promise."

He emerged from the master bedroom and scanned the living room, front door, back door, and the arched glass windows on both sides of the house. Without thinking much, he took quick strides across the living room to reach the girl, who gazed at him with eyes wide open in fear. He smiled a little and said, "Don't worry," before cutting the nylon ropes using the sharp knife he had pulled from the side of his robe.

Maya sat still and looked straight at him. Her eyes searched for answers.

"Are you a good man or a bad man?" she asked.

The innocence in her voice brought a smile to Harrison's face in spite of the burning pain in his dog-bitten leg. "It depends."

"You silly, I am not very good at solving puzzles, okay? Please tell me." She cocked her head slightly to her left. "Are you a good man or bad man?"

You silly.

"I am a good guy. My name is Harrison. What is yours?"

"Maya. I want to go home." She looked sideways as if to see if someone was there.

"Don't worry, Maya. Are you scared?" He continued to scan the front and back doors.

"My mom told me to be brave all the time. I am brave." She paused before adding, "Little scared though. Are you scared too?" Maya gazed at the long blade he was holding.

Harrison nodded as he coiled the long blade into a belt. "Yes, I am scared too. Don't worry. I will get you out of this place. If both of us are brave, we can save the other girls locked up in a barn behind this house."

"Other girls?" Maya's eyes widened.

"I will explain later." Harrison extended his left arm to help Maya get up.

"What about the man with the glasses?" Maya tried to balance herself as she got up. Her legs were numb.

"I don't know. He may be waiting near that door." He pointed at the back door, slightly turning to his right. "Or—"

He quickly turned left at the sound of broken glass and felt the pain in his stomach. He spotted the broken window and glass pieces scattered below as he fell down onto the floor a few inches away from the leather couch.

Maya screamed.

Thomas rode his wheelchair through the front door. His left hand operated the wheelchair and his right hand pointed a Glock 9mm at Harrison. Excessive sweat dripped down from his forehead through his eyelashes and down to his neck. His windpipe narrowed and gave a whistling sound as he breathed hard. The only thing he wanted now was to empty the Glock chamber into the guy lying down on the floor.

In a fraction of a second, Harrison bent his knees toward his stomach, lifted himself off the floor, and whirled the long steel blade weapon at Thomas. As the blade came back to him after slashing Thomas's face and shoulder, he got up and stood straight.

Thomas panicked and fired. The shot missed the target by a few inches and hit Harrison's naval.

Harrison whirled the blade again at Thomas's right wrist. The 9mm fell onto the floor. Thomas ignored the burning sensation in his right hand and drove the wheelchair straight at Harrison in an effort to knock him down.

Harrison moved to his left and wrapped his right arm around Thomas's neck as the wheelchair passed by on his right. He snapped his neck in a blink.

The wheelchair holding the dead man hit the wall and whirred.

Maya screamed. "He shot you! He shot you—" She ran toward him.

"It's okay. You are safe now." He looked down at his bleeding stomach. There were multiple shots in his abdomen. He felt an excruciating burning sensation in his stomach and hip. *Not looking good.*

Harrison felt dizzy as he slowly walked toward the couch. Maya held his hands and helped him to sit down. "How do we stop this blood? How do we stop it? Are you going to die? Please don't die."

Harrison smiled at Maya, who kept talking.

"What should I do? How can you smile? Are you not feeling the pain?" Maya held his hand and looked around in fear and confusion.

"I smile because you are safe now. No one can hurt you."

Tears formed in her eyes as she noticed the blood coming out of his nose. "We need to go to the hospital. Do you have a phone? We need to call the ambulance."

He nodded, reached under his robe, and retrieved the phone. "Don't worry about me. Listen…Be brave, okay?" He looked into Maya's eyes. Then, he dialed 911.

"My name is Harrison. I found the guys who kidnapped many girls in the Bay Area. Send the cops to Erskine Ranch in Woodside." He paused for a moment. "One more thing…call the FBI and let special agent Theaker know. It's important."

He sighed as he clicked the end button. He turned to his right and smiled at Maya, who leaned her head against his right shoulder. She looked up and stared into his eyes. Her tears trickled down her cheek.

"Don't worry. You will be fine. The cops are on their way."

"I'm not worried about me. I'm worried about *you*. I'm scared. Are you going to die? Who are you?"

"I am a father to a brilliant girl like you."

Maya sat up straight. "You have a daughter? What's her name?"

"April," Harrison said as he took out the heart-shaped pendant wrapped around his neck and clicked open the latch to reveal the picture. "Here she is!"

"She looks beautiful." Maya smiled. Her tear-filled eyes lit up.

"Yeah, she is." The burning sensation spread from his stomach to his chest. He sighed. "When the cops come in, make sure you tell them everything that happened here. Ask them to search the barn. Can you do that, please?"

Maya nodded. She hugged him. "Thank you. You are a good man!" Her teary eyes twinkled, and a tiny dimple appeared in her cheek.

Harrison laughed. He forgot the intense pain in his abdomen for a few seconds. He had not laughed heartily for years.

Maya looked up and smiled wryly as he laughed.

He wiped away tears of joy and called Russell Edison. He spoke for a few minutes. He paused for a second to control his breathing before concluding the conversation. "I may not see you again. Thank you, Russell. Good-bye." He ended the call without waiting for a reply.

Two minutes later, Harrison took a deep breath as he heard the police sirens in the distance.

"I think the cops are almost here. They may be storming in. Don't be scared, okay? Just stay on the couch. Remember, your mom is right. You are a very brave girl. Got it?"

Maya nodded slightly without lifting her head off his shoulder.

Harrison felt his heartbeat slowing down. His feet were cold. He saw Taryn holding April's hand. He was calm and peaceful now.

He held the pendant in his right palm and smiled at April's picture. Then, he took a deep breath and closed his eyes.

Epilogue

It was fifteen minutes past seven o'clock in the evening. Sheriff Scarski adjusted the brim of his glasses and stared at the dead man lying close to the back door, in the middle of dark blood. Then, he looked up at the dim light at the entrance of the barn visible through the window before turning to Agent Theaker and Samantha Cruz. "These bastards did all these horrible things right under our nose. We missed it. I feel terrible." His voice reflected sincere apology.

Theaker nodded without saying a word. He spoke after a brief moment. "I have seen horrible crimes in the last fifteen years, but this—this is the worst, cruelest. These bastards are animals. They tortured these girls—one of them is just four." He sighed and turned to see Agent Jones on his right.

"Sorry, I was tied up in North Bay. What exactly happened here? Twelve girls were locked up here?" Jones leaned against the bar stool, shook his head, and threw up his hands.

"Yes. Twelve girls, including Emily Turner, the girl who

was kidnapped in Foster City... Here is what happened. This guy—" Theaker pointed at the man facing the ceiling with his dead eyes, "Bob McFarlane—this guy's father worked for that man." Now, he pointed at the man riding an Arabian horse in the large portrait hung on the wall. "That man is none other than Gary Erskine, a multimillionaire, who made his fortune in horse racing and cattle farming. Bob's father worked for Erskine's cattle farm in San Fernando. Bob's parents were killed in the earthquake in 1971. He was fifteen by then. Erskine brought the young boy into his fold and brought him here to take care of the horses."

Jones raised his hand. "How do we know all this?"

"Well, come here…" Theaker signaled Jones as he walked over to his right and pointed at the pale-brown notebooks spread on the dining table. "These are all diaries…Bob McFarlane's diaries. Samantha found these in his closet. I read only part of it. Anyways, Gary Erskine's son and daughter-in-law died in an Air France accident in Paris in 1989. The couple had a son, Thomas Erskine, who was five at that time. A year later, Gary Erskine died. Since then, Bob has been the guardian for Thomas." He paused for a moment before continuing, "Thomas was diagnosed with a growth disorder. Bob treated Thomas like his own son— well, I guess all this wealth helped along with his loyalty." He looked at the barn before adding, "Bob was teaching Thomas to ride when he was seventeen. An Arabian horse, the favorite horse of his grandfather, rolled over on young Thomas and crushed his legs. Bob got so pissed off that he shot all the horses and buried them under the barn."

He took a deep breath. "Then, he did something unthinkable. Walk with me; you need to see this."

Jones, Cruz and Scarski followed Theaker, who passed

two doors on his left and opened the third door. "Thomas was thirty-one, but look at all these costumes," he said as he opened the wooden almirah. "The guy wore a Superman costume and forced the girls to wear Rapunzel costumes while he raped them. Sick bastard." He kicked the empty mattress on his right in sheer anger and frustration. "He was infatuated with young girls. He behaved and acted like a young boy stuck in his teens due to his mental disorder. Apparently, he wanted to *grow up* with the girls before marrying them." He shook his head in disgust. "Bob McFarlane fueled Thomas Erskine's fantasy by kidnapping the girls and fed his need for dominance. These snakes spit their venom on so many innocent girls."

~

Russell Edison replayed the phone conversation he had had with Harrison as he drove toward Atherton. *Harry was here the whole time?* He shook his head in disbelief.

An hour later, he pulled into the circular driveway before a Victorian house in Atherton. The house looked smaller compared to the mansions owned by dot-com billionaires surrounding it. Two police vehicles were parked on the side, and a black Chevy Tahoe with an FBI decal was parked closer to the front entrance.

Russell parked his Lexus behind the FBI vehicle, took a deep breath, and looked at the dark, cloudy sky above. *Please God, let him be alive.*

As he walked into the hallway and to the living room, he spotted the two agents who were combing through the bookshelves on the right side wall. A giant Buddha statue in the middle of the living room smiled at him. To his right, an agent with a dark-blue FBI coat raised his brow as he came down the stairs.

"I am here to meet with Agent Theaker. Harrison asked me to come here." Russell took a sleek business card from his coat pocket and handed it to the agent.

"I'm Theaker." The agent shook his hand.

"Is Harrison alive? Where is he?" Russell was anxious.

Theaker folded his lips and shook his head sideways. "Sorry. Harrison is dead."

Russell clutched his chest, walked slowly toward the small couch on his right, and lowered himself onto the couch as he sobbed. Theaker sat next to him and spoke after a minute. "Harrison asked you to meet with me?"

Russell nodded as he wiped away his tears. "Yes. I have been his friend since college days. Poor Harry went through a lot of tragedies. Taryn, his wife, was killed in the September Eleventh terrorist attack. His daughter, April, was kidnapped and killed in 2004." He felt a lump in his throat and struggled to speak.

"April Azevedo?" Theaker widened his eyes in sadness. "I was the lead investigator in her kidnapping. Her death saddened me beyond words." He paused for a moment. "I remember talking to April's father. The man I knew was very different from the man I found today."

Russell took a deep breath and nodded. "Harry is a gentleman. He did not hurt anyone. He was so kind. But—" He sobbed. "Tragedy struck him twice. After April was gone, he was devastated. He could not focus on the company, Yosemite Networks, he founded. He promoted me as CEO and left the country. He is still the biggest shareholder of the company. But we had no idea where he was."

He stared at the Buddha statue and continued, "A year

after he left, he called me from Tibet. He became a Buddhist monk. All these years, we have been communicating through Skype and emails. He was in Tibet for many years, India for a couple of years, and then Israel." He took a deep breath. "But I didn't know he had come back to the United States. All of us thought that he was still somewhere in Asia."

He took a minute to compose himself and said, "Harrison called me three hours ago. I was in an offsite meeting in Monterey. He told me that his time had come. He gave me the address of this house and asked me to come here to meet with you. He told me that he had prepared something for the FBI. It should be here…" He walked closer to the Buddha statue, pushed a bronze button on the side, pulled a rusted copper door below the statue, and found a white DVD sleeve. "For the FBI" was written on the DVD.

A few minutes later, Theaker pushed the DVD into his Mac laptop and watched Harrison appearing on the screen. He had a clean-shaven head and sad, reddish eyes as if he had not slept for weeks. He looked straight at the camera.

"If you are watching this, I am dead. I should have been dead a long time ago—when Taryn died. I wanted to live because of my little angel. She was also taken from me by a cruel bastard." He looked up at the ceiling and paused for a few seconds. "I had no reason to live after April was gone. I went all over the world searching for the meaning of this life. I spent six years in Tibet. One day, I determined that what happened to April should not happen to other children. I decided to do what you guys…" He pointed at the camera. "…you guys—FBI, cops, law enforcement, and the justice system—failed to do."

Russell looked at Theaker, who was staring at the screen.

"Why it is so difficult to stop child abductions in this

country?" He paused. "*Because* there is no serious punishment for these crimes. All these criminals should be killed as soon as they are caught. Not just killed, they should be tortured and killed just the way these bastards killed the young, innocent children. Each and every child killer out there should realize there is a serious punishment for their crimes. Even the thought of abducting children should send a chill up their spines. They should feel the fear. *Then only*, they will stop. This menace will stop." His piercing eyes stared at the camera.

"I decided to serve justice. Not just that, I decided to prevent the crime before it happened. I spent many years preparing myself for that. I learned martial arts from the monks in Tibet. I spent two years in Israel to learn Krav Maga and weapons. I became a one-man army and came back here two years ago. I trolled underground websites and found the pedophiles, and I took them out one by one. I do not have the count of how many crooks I took off the street. That count goes up every week, unfortunately. However…it's not a question of how many crooks I killed; it's a question of how many young children I saved. I wish that every parent who lost their children to the monsters would *do something* to teach a lesson to those monsters."

Harrison stood up and stopped the recording.

Thank You

Thank you for taking the time to read *Tell My Dad*. If you liked it, please consider telling your friends or posting a short review on Amazon, Goodreads, or wherever you purchased it. Word of mouth is an author's best friend and much appreciated.

Ram Muthiah